Hustle Made:
The Bitch, The Life and The Streets

A Novel By:

T. Marie

Eclectic Publishing LLC.

eclecticpublishingllc@gmail.com

Cover Design 2016 By Marc Wilkins

The characters and events portrayed in this book are fictitious. Any similarity to real persons, living or dead is purely coincidental and not intended by the author.

ISBN-13: 978-0998542904
ISBN-10: 0998542903

Dedication

This is for everyone with a dream. Reach past the stars!!!

Chapter One

Bang. Bang Bang!!!! It was the loudest gunshot I ever heard. My ears rung. I saw the small amount of smoke from the chamber of the millennium forty-five. I smelled the powder from the bullet. I was stuck. I couldn't move, I was in shock.

When I finally blinked and snapped out of my daze I realized I had blood all over me. It was in my mouth and I could feel it all over my face. It felt warm and thick, but it didn't have a smell. I looked up at Enoch, who stood right at six foot even, and saw a look of rage and pure hate in his eyes. "What the fuck did you do?" I was finally able to get out. I was so shocked at what had just happened.

I was confused. I was confused as fuck! Enoch had gotten out of control and the shit he got us into was real fucked up. I couldn't get it together. I was shaking and shivering like I was cold. I felt like I was going to throw the fuck up. I could hardly move. It was like my body was cement. Like I had bricks in my shoes. I looked down at my hands it was even more blood and they shook like crazy, too.

Blood was everywhere. Blood was on my shoes. My hair. My arms. My heart pounded. It was so hard to catch my breath. I didn't know what to do next. Despite Enoch yelling the directions to me, I still couldn't figure it out. I couldn't function. I was caught completely off guard.

Enoch screamed at me again, "Karter wash the fucking blood off of you now man!!! We gotta get the fuck outta here." He foamed at the mouth. I saw golds on his teeth along with white shit around his lips and in the corner of his mouth. He was way gone and I was a nervous fucking wreck.

I kept trying to talk myself into moving faster. I kept trying to tell myself I was tripping. I kept trying to tell myself I was dreaming. This was all bad. Like really bad. I didn't think Enoch understood what kind of bullshit he put us in.

I still could hardly catch my breath. I tried to calm down so I could think straight. My mind was going a million miles a second. I played so many things over in my head. I tried to figure out why that had just happened. I still couldn't believe it had.

As I looked down at the lifeless male's body, lying on the floor in a pool of his own blood I noticed his size. He looked small laying on the floor. When he was alive he was a huge guy. He had belly and all. But, he looked tiny as hell with no life in him.

How the hell did this happen? We were supposed to go by his homeboy's house like we had done time and time again. Chill, get something, smoke something, and use the restroom. Shit we've even had orgies with him and his girl. His house was our house when we were in town. It was not at all supposed to have happened that way.

What I didn't know was why? Why did feel the need to take his life? What the fuck was so fucked up between them that he killed his homie? This shit was fucked up!!! It was all I kept thinking. I also kept thinking I had to get far the fuck away from there!!!! And fast!!!

Enoch must have gotten himself into some bullshit or done something scandalous to the homie. Why else would he have taken his life? We did licks and set mutha fuckas up. We ran off with money, robbed, and stole. But, that was some shit that I wasn't able to comprehend. *Not the homie!*

"BITCH! Come the fuck on. You taking all mutha fucking day. We ain't got time for yo dumb ass to be moving slow. Snap the fuck out of it and let's get the fuck up outta here." Enoch yelled at me with a black trash bag in his hand.

He moved around the room frantic and nervous. He tried to be as cautious as he could. He needed to be though. He needed to be scared like me, but the fact that he had just knocked off his partner didn't even phase him. He handed me the bag and told me to take everything off and put it in there. I did as I was told, even though it made no sense to me, I obliged.

The nigga that was just murked was a solid nigga. He was also a BOSS because he had that cake. But, the most fucked up part of it all was it was Enoch 's mutha fuckin partner!

Those two grew up together, took care of each other, and the whole nine. He was the reason we were in Dallas any fuckin way. I couldn't believe this shit happened. Man, it was fucked up!

I knew Enoch was way gone off the drugs and alcohol. Desperate as hell, but I didn't know it was to that extent. Was it something else that made him take his friend's life? I clearly stayed too fucking high my damn self to see he was headed for self-destruction.

Enoch had done some scandalous shit. He wasn't right at all and I was right there with him doing it. But the thing about it was he never crossed the Fam. NEVER. That was something that he said he would never do. I guess when you are strung out, broke, and jealous you would do any damn thing.

Enoch disappeared yet again from the front room where I stood and the home boy laid dead. *What the fuck was he doing?* I asked myself. My ears began to ring again. Maybe they never stopped. How would we explain this shit? How in the hell would we go on like this had never happened?

That showed me just how far Enoch was gone. He didn't care who he hurt or what he did. All he wanted was drugs and money. That let me know that I needed to get the fuck away from him and fast. I needed a bump. I needed a drag. I needed some type of drug in my blood stream right at that moment because I felt like I went crazy. I felt like I was in the twilight zone or something. Like I had an out of body experience.

I had seen dead bodies before. I done even shot niggas before. I've seen blood and guts. I robbed a nigga before. I made a nigga get ass naked and dropped his ass of miles away from his city. I had done a lot of shit and seen a lot of shit, but that right there was the first for me.

I had never seen a nigga kill his homeboy for some shit his boy would have just given him. I had never seen a nigga so desperate he would kill the very nigga who looked out for him. I had never seen another person hate somebody they were close to so much that they wanted them dead. But, I did that day.

Enoch came back into the room with two large Gucci duffle bags. He didn't look spooked anymore at that point. He had a strange look on his face. He looked at me with a look of achievement. He looked at me with the look of accomplishment. He even seemed to walk with his chest out. He looked as if he was proud of what he had just did. But, did he not understand how much bullshit he put us in?

Did he not know that it was his fucking boy he knocked the fuck off? I didn't know what was going on with Enoch, but I knew right then and there that if I didn't get the fuck away from him that he or I would end up just like ole boy. Dead as a fucking door knob.

We make our way to the car as the birds chirped. I started to listen and no sirens or anything. I was surprised about that because I was sure somebody besides us heard the shots.

That wasn't at all a poor neighborhood where they heard shots all the time and didn't think anything of it. It puzzled me, but not enough to stay around to try and find out if they had been called or not.

As we drove I couldn't help but cry. I never cried. I rarely showed emotion. Whether shit went bad or good I checked my feelings and kept it moving. Yet that right there was different.

It wasn't just any ole person or bullshit we had done. It wasn't even in the plans. Not in the plans at all. We just went to the home boys house for the normal shit. But when we got there things took a completely different turn.

I was scared to talk to Enoch. I didn't say a word for a long time. Even after I cried I still didn't talk to him. He did nothing to console me either. He just turned the music up and made his way to I-35E N. I wondered when he would talk to me about what happened.

I wondered when he would tell me why he did what he did. I wondered how he felt. I wondered what he thought. I wondered when he would ask me if I was okay. I wondered when he would tell me things would be okay. The sad part was he never explained any of what I wondered about.

Enoch simply handed me the little brown bottle that contained the coke he and I both couldn't function without. I unscrewed the top, placed a bit on my hand and snorted it. I repeated those same steps two more times until I was able to fully relax.

I was on my level then. I laid my head back on the head rest and stared at the cars driving in front of me. I zoned out as we continued down the highway headed straight to Kansas City. Missouri that is. The town where it goes down. The show me state. Killer City. Misery!

I was born and raised in Kansas City had never lived anywhere else so I took full advantage of any chance I could get to get away from that bitch. But, when I made it home from all that bullshit we were just involved in I was happier than a john in a whore house.

Finally, home. Finally! I kept thinking to myself that no one would find out about old boy we had left dead. I hoped that they would just chop it up as a robbery gone bad.

I hoped that I would never have to mention, speak, or even think about the ordeal ever again. But, I knew that day would come. It was inevitable. I tried to move on with life as usual, but it was hard. I found myself depressed and sick as a damn dog. I was literally in the house for weeks. All I did was smoke, snort, try to eat, and throw up.

I wanted that scene out of my head. I wanted all the guilt I felt to go away. I wanted to be numb to all of my feelings. I wanted to stop feeling the hurt I allowed Enoch to cause me. I wanted to feel happy.

I wanted to get rid of all the bullshit that happened to me growing up and the shit that was going on right then. I wanted to erase any memory of my mother. I wanted to erase the memory of just killing my friend. I wanted to never remember the fuckery I had to deal with in my life period. I tried, but no matter what I did I woke up to the same ole fucked up reality.

Chapter Two

Ring. Ring. Ring. The phone rung and woke me up out of my sleep. I looked on the bed at my phone, not ringing. It starts up again. Ring. Ring. Ring. It was his phone in his Carhart coat that hung on the door of the closet which was not far from me.

Ring. Ring. Ring. It was louder at that point. I dug in the pockets and retrieved the phone, slid the phone to talk and put it to my ear. It was some bitch, talking to somebody in the background. I said hello and she hung up. The number that was in the caller ID I knew, I had seen it in his phone before. I make a mental note of the number.

Then, the bitch called back. The second time, she got some balls because she didn't hang up. She talked to me like we were cool or something, or like I knew her.

"Karter, where Enoch at?" she says.

"Who is this?" I ask her.

"Girl you know who this is!" She says back.

"Who the fuck is this?" I asked.

"Bitch, just put my man on the phone!" the chick snaps back.

"Yo man! Ha! Bitch, you got the wrong, Enoch." I tell her, laughing.

"You wish I had the wrong one. Where you think he been for all this time? Yep that's right with me and his son you dumb ass hoe," she replies.

She was right about one thing. I really hadn't seen Enoch. Since we had been back from Dallas he was MIA. I saw him twice maybe, three times during the weeks we had been back.

When I saw him all he did was come get money or dope. He would leave some out for me. Do some lines with me as well. Shit maybe even fuck me. Shower and change and then roll right the fuck back out.

He said he wanted to lay low and it would be safer for me if he just stayed away. I cared, but then again, I didn't. I was sick and addicted so I had no time or energy to waste on his crazy no good ass.

Plus, it actually made me feel worse being around him. I was already unhappy and just the presence of him made me depressed. But, after hearing what this bitch said on this phone call and thinking about what he did a few weeks before he had me too fucked up.

Kids!? What the fuck did she just say. "Enoch ain't got no kids by yo trifling ass, bitch. You damn sure ain't his woman, bitch, cause you talking to the one and only hoe!" I was screaming to the top of my lungs. I was pissed. Enoch had done a lot more than I thought.

"Ah bitch, you are as dumb as you look!" She laughed.

"You got a lot to learn and let's start with this first lesson. Enoch is a street nigga and you sure as hell can't change him. On top of the fact I'm not ever going anywhere, bitch!!"

With that she hung up in my face still not revealing to me who the fuck she was.

I turned to head toward the bathroom and ran straight into Enoch with his phone still in my hand. Answering his phone or hell even touching it without permission was like forbidden. He knew he wasn't right and so did I. I didn't want to accept it. I believed it, though. Maybe I should have. It wasn't shit about Enoch that was right.

I looked him straight in his eyes and asked, "Who is she? Who is the bitch you were with all week? And you got more kids? Kids I don't know about? What the fuck, Enoch? Were you ever gon' tell me? Fuck! How many more do you have?"

I managed to get that out in one breath. I was pissed. This nigga didn't stop with his antics. He snatches his phone from my hand and pushes me so hard to the floor that I flew across it. Then he said, "I don't have to explain shit to you! You brought this on yourself. You invaded my privacy and answered my phone."

"I told you your place so stay in it. Don't question me about what the fuck I do or where I'm at. None of that shit. I'm a grown ass man, bitch. If you don't like it, you can leave this muthafucka. Besides ain't you tired of letting them bitches get you all worked up for nothing yet!?"

The nigga was cocky! Cocky as fuck! He acted like I had no choice but to stay with him. He had me and life fucked up. *I didn't have to deal with his cheating, snorting, killing, robbing, and stealing, no good, woman beating, hella kid having ass! Like he was doing me a favor.*

Fuck him and those bitches and all the bullshit he had put me through. He was way too damn comfortable. First, he offs his friend now more kids. What else don't I know about Enoch?

Some niggas think that if they help you or do a little bit for you, that you are to take all the bullshit they dish out. Fuck that!!! That was straight bullshit. Hell I did just as much as he did, if not more to bring money into that bitch. I was the one setting up niggas, making drops, and anything else he told me to do. I did any and everything for Enoch.

I risked my life on a regular basis. I made sure I was nothing but loyal to him and that nigga wanted to keep doing the fool. Fuck him and the horse he rode in on. I wasn't about to keep taking that shit from that dude. I was tired of being controlled by that dope he kept feeding me.

I was tired of getting the shit beat out of me for no explanation at all. I was sure as hell tired as fuck of his cheating ass, fucking anything with a slit. On top of the fact I didn't know what he was going to do at any point because he was so gone off of that "smack". I was tired of Enoch and I was tired of living like this.

If he thought I was going to keep taking it he was sadly mistaken. "I don't get myself worked up for nothing!!!! I'm tired of going through this shit with you, Enoch! Why can't you just be a fucking man!? I don't deserve this bullshit from you or no other nigga! Fuck you, with yo no good ass!! You know what you are, You a FUCK BOY!" I said as I got up off the floor.

The entire time I yelled and screamed he was getting dressed. He was popping tags, lacing new kicks, and topped it all off with the KC hat to match. But, when I said 'fuck boy' he stood up from the edge of the bed and grabbed me by my neck with both of his hands.

He held me up in the air while he squeezed my neck. I put my hands around his, trying to get him to let go. I scratched and grabbed at his arms and hands. It did nothing. *This nigga is trying to kill me!*

My legs and feet dangled below me. I could not breath. No matter how hard I tried I couldn't take a breath. No matter how hard I scratched and grabbed his hands, he wouldn't let go. He just kept screaming at me.

"Bitch, you got me fucked up! Who the fuck you think I am?"

He was so mad I could see the rage and anger in his eyes. Every time he said a word I could feel the warm spit hit my face, but I couldn't make out what the words were any longer. I was beginning to fade away.

I could no longer keep my eyes open and I didn't have any more strength to kick, grab, or even move. The lack of oxygen took its toll on me. I felt really sleepy. My eyes closed and I couldn't open them back up. I didn't hear anything else.

I didn't feel anything else. It was like I was in a different world or something. Like I was in another universe. It almost felt like that first high I felt when Enoch gave me that blunt laced with coke. *"I must be dead,"* I said to myself.

Just as I started to feel I was drifting away even more, I hit the floor. A few seconds later I could hear footsteps, and then the door slam. My air way was finally free.

I still couldn't open my eyes, but I continued to cough and grasp for air. It was like I was alive again. I coughed more, and then started breathing normally again. I started to cry and cry. Mentally and emotionally, I was fucked up.

I thought to myself, *What is wrong with me? What did I do to make him stay away? Did I not do something right? Did I make him mad? What is wrong with me? Why did he always put his hands on me? Why does he hate me? Why am I still here? Why couldn't I just leave his ass?!*

I snapped out of that self-pity shit fast. *Fuck Enoch.* I thought. Enoch had really gotten beside himself. It was amazing how the more money nigga's get the more bitches and drama it brings. Then, they head gets even bigger. On top of it all, they think that the money can fix everything.

He was the perfect example. I just wanted to know how he would do all this shit without me? How would he make all this money without me? I got up and looked at my neck in the dresser mirror. You could see marks around my next. My vision was blurry in one eye, but I could for sure tell I had hand prints on my damn neck. *He was literally trying to fucking kill me!*

There was no way I would be able to keep dealing with that from him. One, if not both of us would end up dead by the hands of the other. That was not at all okay with me, but I knew it was my reality if I stayed. The thing was I didn't have shit but clothes, shoes, and a car. I didn't have any money, any savings, or a stash. Nothing.

I had no family I could go to because they weren't worth shit. I had no clue where my punk-ass-dope-fiend mother was and I didn't know for sure who my father was.

I had enough of thinking this or that person was him, and then, turned out not to be my father after he tried to fuck me or ended up molesting me. My fucked up ass momma tried to get paid and get a hit of whatever she was using at the time. Fuck that shit, too.

As I tried to think of what I would do, I found the dope and sprinkled some out on the mirror that was on the dresser I stood in front of. I chopped it up into a few lines to snort. I stared at myself in the mirror a little longer. I stared and I got nothing back from myself. I felt empty inside. I felt like a crab shell with no meat on the inside.

I couldn't think anymore because my thoughts began to just jumble together. I snorted my first line. Sniff. Sniff. I took my second line. Sniff. Sniff. I took the third line. Sniff. Sniff.

I wanted to take another line, but as I looked at myself in the mirror again I saw my mother staring back at me. Here I am 24 years old and I was a split fucking image of her. I hated her with a passion. I wanted so bad to be better than her but really I was worse.

I hit the mirror and screamed at her. You bitch!!! All THIS IS YOUR FUCKING FAULT. I said it to her but I was really talking to myself. I was looking right back at myself. If I didn't change I would end up just like her. I threw myself on the bed and started to cry again. I laid in the fetal position and cried more and more until I cried myself to sleep.

Chapter Three

When I woke up, it was the next day. It was the end of fall so there were no birds chirping. No warm sun rays shining through the window. It was grey, cold, and gloomy outside, which matched exactly how I felt that time.

The first thing I did when I got up was run to the bathroom to hurl. That had been my routine since we had gotten back from Dallas. I stayed in the house all those weeks, not only because I was spooked, but I was also sick as hell. I just chopped it up to the dope.

After I brushed my teeth and swished with mouth wash, I went to the dresser where I left the dope from the day before on the mirror and snorted the remaining two lines. I looked in the newly broken mirror again and said to myself, *"You gone end up just like her."*

I started to look around the standard sized fully furnished room that I had been in for weeks. I looked at the floor, which had clothes and shoes all over it. I look at the dresser that was full of cups, fast food bags, ashtrays, and the mirror for the dope. That room was a fucking disaster and I was living right in the filth!!! I didn't attempt to move or pick up shit. I simply just sprinkled out more dope, made more lines, and snorted more it.

I loved the way the dope made me feel. It made me feel numb and free. It made me forget about all the bullshit that I had done and been through. I wanted to keep that feeling forever. I wanted to be numb to the fucked up world I lived in.

I wanted to just forget about it all; for it to never enter my memory again. I sat on the edge of the bed and came to the conclusion that I was going to get out of that fucking room that day. I would get out of that damn house. I had been down for a long time.

I checked in the top drawer of the dresser, where Enoch always left me some change, to see what I was working with. I didn't see anything. I moved stuff around and nothing. Then, I became frantic because there was no more coke left there, either.

That pussy! It's cool, though. I wondered what the hell I would do. I wondered what he was doing and where he was. I hated to even say it, but Enoch was right about one thing. I did get myself all worked up and did absolutely nothing, but stay right there with him taking everything he dished out.

I started to feel a little queasy. My stomach was upset and I couldn't understand why I continued to feel like this. I previously just thought it was due to the dope. I thought it was because I started using more and more and my tolerance level was extremely high. I assumed that the feelings of sickness and stuff were because all I did most of the time was snort dope. I didn't even eat really.

The times I did eat, it was a fucking kids meal or something from somewhere. That didn't stop me from throwing the shit right back up though. I was tired of being sick. I wanted to know what the fuck was going on but I was to preoccupied with the bastard Enoch and the dope he took from me.

This wasn't the first time a bitch had confirmed what intuition had already told me. That wasn't the first time he had put his hands on me and acted like there wasn't a thing wrong with it. That wasn't the first time he had been gone for days at a time.

That wasn't the first time for any of his shenanigans and it for damn sure wasn't about the be the last. That was if I didn't do what I should have done a long time ago and leave his bitch ass.

I knew I needed to, but I couldn't. I knew I shouldn't have stayed there any longer, but I had nowhere else to go. Who was going to give me money? Who would get my dope?

Who was I going to rob these busters with? Who would be my getaway driver? How was I going to do this shit alone? How? *No. You don't wanna live like that anymore, Karter.* I said to myself. I needed to get out of the game not stay in it.

I shook that self-pity off once again. I got dressed, and got out of that damn house. I grabbed my LV duffle bag and put a few items in it just in case I didn't make it back that night and left.

I wasn't sure where I would go, but I knew I needed to get out of that miserable ass house. I made sure I had my heat, got the little money and dope that I had stashed and I was out that bitch.

As I walked out of the door I told Bunny that I was leaving and I would check on her after a while. She didn't care either way. Her stories were on and she had a bowl of popcorn in her lap. She was addicted to those things. She didn't even look away from the television.

Bunny was a friend of the family who ended up raising Enoch. She raised him like her grandson. His mother was too young to even know what she was getting herself into nor how to handle the situation.

She was raped by her uncle and was scared to tell. She knew her mother wouldn't believe her either. Since Bunny was a friend of her family who she trusted, she told her everything. So when she ended up at Bunny house, pregnant, she took her in.

After Enoch was born, his mother left and left Enoch there. She wanted to finish school and get a job then come back for Enoch. That's not at all how it worked out.

She never came back for Enoch so Bunny had a grandson. In fact, Bunny never heard from her again because the uncle killed her. After I found all of that out I understood why Enoch was so fucked up.

I tossed my bag and purse in the back of my 09 Camaro and backed out of the driveway. It was cold. It felt like it would snow at any minute, yet it was only the Fall season. As I drove I had no real destination in mind, but the ride was good since I hadn't been out of the house for so long.

I needed a bump, but I knew that I didn't have much left, so I needed it to last until I found a nigga to rob for it or one to give it to me. I wasn't about to buy no damn coke. Fuck that! I opened my ashtray and found just what I needed. A blunt. I lit it immediately. I smoked and continued to drive.

As I gripped the wheel I noticed my hands slightly shaking. I needed a fix. I needed to get my life in order and strung out on coke was not about to help that. I would have had to keep doing schemes and licks to keep up with the habit I had.

But at the same time I didn't even want to be on that shit forreal. I seen what it did to Enoch and I did not want to end up like that. I didn't want to be so gone out of my mind I would take the life of a nigga I called fam. I didn't want to be like my mother and let the people I cared about be taken advantage of either.

At that point I was tired of the game all together. I was tired of having to pack heat everywhere I went. I was tired of having to rob and steal from people. I was tired of traveling to cities letting men take advantage of me just to jack them.

I was sick of snorting this coke up my nose every five minutes, chasing that high I had the first day Enoch gave it to me in a laced blunt. I was sick of this bullshit life I was so called living. But really, I wasn't even living. I didn't know what I would do. I was just a puppet for this no good ass nigga who didn't deserve me at all.

I drove around the city, smoking my blunt while my mind wondered. I ended up at the light on 63rd and Prospect. I was facing north on Prospect. I was in a daze, waiting for the light to change so I could make my left turn. The weed had worked my appetite up and I was craving some Mad Jacks.

I hadn't been able to keep anything down in days, but that Mad Jacks sounded good at that moment. Next thing I knew this black Benz coupe pulled up next to me, slamming! I looked to my right and couldn't see a damn thing. It has some of that none-of-your-business tint and the car was fresh as hell.

I got the green arrow so I made my left turn. I proceeded on my journey to cure my hunger. I looked up in my rearview and noticed the Benz was, at that point, right behind me; as if it was following me. I thought nothing of it at first.

I just assumed they were going somewhere in the same area, but then again the car wasn't in the turning lane at first. I should have caught onto that way sooner. I was really off of my square. Just so out of it. I knew that the situation could have turned really bad.

All the shit Enoch and I had done caused me to have no idea at all about who was in that car. Next thing I knew the Benz was right on my ass. *What the fuck? This car is following me.* My heart started to beat fast. Then, I thought that it was Nice people.

Nice was the friend Enoch knocked off in Dallas. Nice was the nigga he shot and killed and left lying in his own house in a pool of his own blood. That was some shit I still had a hard time wrapping my mind around.

I sped up so did the Benz. I grabbed my heat from under my seat. As I steered with my knee I put the clip in and cocked it to make sure it was one in head. I laid it on my lap and started to look out my rear view mirrors again.

I wanted to turn off and see if they would as well, but thought twice about it. That would have been a bad set up for me. *Pull in the police station. Fuck no Karter. So, you can be arrested for having this pistol that's not registered to you.* I was having a talk with myself to figure out what the hell to do next.

That shit had me spooked. I wasn't sure of my next moves. I wasn't for sure of who was in that car. I slowed down to see what they were going to do. I didn't take my hand off that trigger. I was for sure going to bust at they ass first, whoever the fuck it was.

Fuck it! I decided to turn inside the Landing Mall parking lot. I had forgotten all about my growling stomach. I wanted to know who was in the car and why they were on my ass like that. I was ready for whatever they had to give.

As I slowed down I looked in my rear view mirror again. I was preparing to stop. I took my foot off the gas. I wanted the Benz to get close to me so I could slam on my breaks, make them rear end me, and get out letting loose on em.

They didn't fall for the bait. They kept driving. It could have been a coincidence or just my paranoia. Shit that wasn't new, though. I stayed looking over my shoulder. I was sick of the shit, but at the same time I didn't know any better. I stayed parked for a minute. I put my gun on safety and put it under my seat.

Since I was at the landing I decided to get out and kill some time. I could get food and do a little shopping. I grabbed my purse to look for dope so I could take a bump. My nerves were bad and I was paranoid as hell. I was shaking even more. I found my bag, sprinkled some on the back of my hand, and sniffed.

I did that two more times before I felt like I was good. I let out a long breath and sat there for a brief minute. I was on my level again now. I proceeded to the landing entrance once I was out of my car. It wasn't many stores in that mall, but you could always find some kicks.

Chapter Four

I walked around the mall for a while, but nothing caught my eye and it didn't take me long to leave. On top of the fact my stomach was growling and didn't like anything that was available there. Soo I quickly left.

I arrived back at my car and as I reached for the car door handle I heard somebody call my name. "KARTER!" I turned and looked to see who it was. It was some chick. I didn't know who she was. She didn't look familiar to me at all.

As she started to walk toward me, I dug my hand in my purse for my heat. But then, I thought about it. I left it in the car under the seat. If it would have been in my bag I would have shot that hoe!! I didn't know her and I had done too much shit to just be friendly to muthafuckas.

Who was the bitch, anyway? Just as I was about to take my hand out of my purse I felt my brass knuckles and slid them on. I was ready for this bitch because she just looked like she was up to no good. I had the feeling some shit was about to go down and boy did it.

"Do I know you?" I ask that bitch. She stood about 5'7 with long weave and a hat on. The bitch was big and she was not cute. "Na, you don't, but Enoch do. I told you before to leave my man alone and you just can't get the picture."

This bitch lunged at me and it seemed like she had something in her hand, but I couldn't see anything but her fist. She started yelling and screaming like a mad woman. She connected a few times on my chest and arm.

I found my in and I let that bitch have it. I punched her right in the face. She was definitely trying to give me a run for my money because she was still going. We were banging like two bitches in a UFC fight. She got me good right on the side of my face too.

I was really pissed. The hoe tried to fuck up my face. She wanted me to be ugly and fucked up like her. I started beating her ass even more and I wasn't going to stop.

We ended up on the ground and I was on top of her. I took all the anger and frustration out on her face and head. All the shit Enoch had done to me I wanted her to feel too!!

I was in a rage and I only stopped when I heard somebody yell "Da po po coming!!" "Po Po coming." I snapped out of that zone and stopped punching her. I got my ass up off the ground and I grabbed my shit from beside my car. I unlocked it, got in, and burned rubber out of that parking lot.

I was pissed all over again. This nigga kept me in some bullshit. Another fight with a bitch I didn't know behind that bitch ass nigga, Enoch. I drove, hitting the steering wheel. I was yelling and screaming at my damn self at that point. I was mad, hurt, and tired.

I looked down at my arms because I felt a burning sensation on them and my chest. I looked down at the sleeves on the hoodie I was wearing and they were soaked in blood. Blood was all over me. I felt my face and looked in the rearview mirror and it was bleeding, too. I headed straight to the hospital.

17 stitches later I was out of the emergency room. During my visit not only did I get sewed up I got some really unexpected news. I was pregnant!! *Damn! Damn! Damn!* I called Enoch like a thousand and one times and he didn't answer.

Not one phone call. I called from the hospital phone and my cousins phone. I texted and everything. Still no answer or response.

Kelly was my cousin and the first person I called when I got to the hospital. It didn't take her long at all to get there. She was present for the pregnant news and all. I'm glad she was there, though. I had had a rough day. Could it have gotten any worse?

When that nurse came back and told me congratulations I thought I was going to pass the hell out. I wasn't ready for no kids. I was strung out on dope, no place to go, and the father of the fetus wasn't worth a damn.

When it was time to leave the hospital Kelly drove me home. One of my arms was really sliced up so I couldn't maneuver the wheel to good. Plus, I was still in shock about this whole pregnancy thing.

I ended up staying with Kelly at her house for a while. Kelly and her sister stayed together in a two-bedroom apartment off of 10th Street and Prospect. Sis was never at home. She was either at work, school.

All I could think about was what I would do with the fetus and how I was gonna shake this dope habit. The stash that I had with me was about gone. I tried my best to make it stretch, but I knew it wasn't going to last much longer.

No matter how much I tried to tell myself that I was in control and could shake that shit, I found myself going right to my little bottle for a bump.

Since stopping right now wasn't going to happen I found myself going back to what I knew best. Taking what the fuck I wanted. I started to peep out the neighborhood where sis stayed while I was there. I wanted to see what hustler was on the corner and what they were slanging.

See, where sis lived was not Beverly Hills. Far from it. It was the inner city. The hood. Straight gutter. I knew I would find exactly what I needed and it wasn't far from where I was laying my head at the time. The corner.

I knew for damn sure I wasn't about to purchase it. I began on my mission. I found out the little' cat who was pushing the corner. I took walks to the liquor store and Humdingers all hours of the day just down the block so I could see what was what.

I knew everything I needed to know in just a few days. I knew their operation. I knew where the trap house was. I knew the runner. I knew the supplier. I knew how and where the corner hustler kept his stash.

In the can on the side of the pole. I knew how I was going to get the young thunder cat on that corner whose dope was in that can! I was gonna rob his ass and rob him blind.

Back to the stealing and jacking. Back to the robbing and taking a niggas shit. Fuck it. I wasn't about to be out there bad and broke. Hell naw! I'm a take that shit from a nigga and whatever else he had that I wanted. The day came where I had no more coke. I had used all my favors and I O U's up.

I had no more tricks or cons and with my habit it didn't take long for me to run out. I tried to let that be my stopping point and quit cold turkey. I tried to just get over the craving and shake it off.

But, when a bitch started shaking and getting sick and I started feeling worse like I was coming down with the flu. I knew I had to get me some dope and I had to get some dope fast.

I had gotten so bad with my habit, I didn't care what form the dope is in. I would have smoked the shit at that point. *FUCK!!!* I needed to get high. Then I thought, *Karter, why don't you just buy some?* Why? I had no idea. I wasn't sure at all. Why didn't I just buy some dope?

I could have purchased some. I had more than enough money to do so. I guess it was a mind thing. I would have really felt like a junkie buying some dope from somebody off the street. Hell nah!

I knew I couldn't keep living like that. I knew I had to change what I did to earn money. I had to find something else to do. It had to be legal or with very minimal risk. The shit I did came with a lot of risk, I had to ask myself was it even worth it.

Looking over your shoulder, paranoia and jail time. Who the fucked wanted to be in the slammer? Nobody. But what I did to earn a living was only going to get me dead or in jail. Period. Was the risk worth the reward?

I had been under 48 hour investigations before, followed, beat up, stabbed, all that. But I kept going back for more. I knew that one day I would be picked up again or worse knocked off.

Maybe I still had enough time to redeem myself. There could still be a small chance I could turn shit around for myself and still be okay. At the same time, I knew that I wouldn't hesitate to take someone's life if mine was in jeopardy.

That night after I took a few shots of Hennessy and smoked a blunt I got dressed in all black. I sat in my car and got my mind right. I started to put my burner gloves on and began to think about Enoch. I hadn't talked to him since he left that day after he choked my ass.

My heart started to beat fast and I began to look around outside the car. I instantly got even more paranoid than usual. I grabbed my gun and turned the safety off. *Why the fuck are you even thinking about him in the first place?* I was pissed at myself for even giving him my energy. But, at the same time I missed him something terrible.

I wanted to see him, I wanted to hug him, I wanted to hear him say some slick shit because that was all that came out of his mouth. I needed my Enoch fix. *What the fuck was wrong with me?*

I picked up the phone and started to push the digits to his number. I was on the 6th number. Ringbzzzzz. Ringbzzzz. Ringbzzzzz. Someone was calling me and my phone was on vibrate and ring at the same time. It was a number I didn't know.

My heart dropped in my stomach. I felt the most butterflies I think I had ever felt. I gagged a little and began to take slow deep breaths. I wasn't sure who it was on the phone and I wanted to know, but I was scared to answer.

Ringbzzzzz. Ringbzzzzz. It went off again. I decided not to answer. I didn't have time for anybody playing on my phone. I didn't have the energy for that shit either. Plus, I was on a mission. *Fuck that phone and fuck Enoch!*

I put the phone in the console of my car and got out. I started to walk to the corner and noticed a random person standing beside a tree on the outside of the gate. I looked around and it seemed I saw more people. It was late so really no reason for so much activity.

The sun was down on a fall night and it was cold, so why the fuck was it so many damn people out there. I was 'noid as fuck and started to trip out. I didn't know why I was so nervous, but I decided not to go through with it. I walked back to my car, got my phone, and went back into sis's house.

Chapter Five

As soon as I walked back into sis's apartment Kelly had some gossip for my ass.

"I got the scoop for yo ass!" She was hyped about something she found out about.

"That chick that you fought, her name is name is Karren. She been fuckin with Enoch for a minute now and she just found out she is pregnant, too, and yes bitch by him. He is over to her spot all the time. She stays in Friendship Village and…"

Kelly went on and on about this and that. She explained that the chic knew about me all along. She knew that I lived with him, how old I was, and the whole nine.

At the same time my girl gave me the low down on that bitch Karren, too. I hadn't said a word the entire time she was talking to me. I was in her room feeling sick as fuck because I needed a fix. I couldn't remember the last time I had eaten and the fetus took all I had.

I was paranoid still about that phone call and all those people all of a sudden. All I wanted to do was get in the bed and under the covers. I wanted to sleep all this shit away!!!

I finally got a chance to ask her how she found all that out. She told me that she did her own little' investigation. She told me that she got most of it from this chick named JaShana. Her baby's daddy had two other kids by this chick named Star. Star was Karren's other baby's daddy cousin. I know some real hood shit!

"Kelly I cannot have this thing growing inside me! I refuse to be caught in a circle like the one you just described." I said. "That's bullshit!!!! No telling how many other kids Enoch has out there and the fact of the matter is he has no respect for me." I began to cry. I was pissed all over again!!! I was emotional, my hormones went wild. And I needed a fucking bump.

Kelly gently grabs my face and turns it to hers. "I say kill the bastard and fuck Enoch! He ain't gone change. He gone leave you with that little fucker while he do him with the next bitch!!! Don't be no damn fool behind that nigga."

I sat there for a minute. I had to process what she said. I was a damn fool for him. I did way too much shit for and with him. What she said sounded real fucked up, but she was being real. It kind of shocked me, but at the same time I needed that.

Hell she had a valid fucking point. She was telling the truth, which was what I tried so hard to escape. Me having a baby wouldn't change shit between us. It sure wouldn't change him.

I'm glad she said what she said because I needed some logical advice and solid support. The way I was thinking was completely opposite. I figured not dealing with it was dealing with it enough. I hoped that somehow it would just go away.

My thinking was totally irrational. Whether or not she agreed with whatever I would decide to do, I knew she was behind me. That helped me. At some point, I would have to come to grips with reality and made a decision. What was the decision I should make? Keep the baby and take care of it by myself or get an abortion?

A few more days past and I hung in there, barely. I was so sick from going through withdrawals I didn't know if I would be able to take it. I finally worked up enough nerve to get the abortion.

I was scheduled to go in the following week. I decided to leave Enoch for good as well. I knew I needed to get all my shit from Bunny's house and that would give me no reason to return. I had to be done with him. And for good.

I hadn't talked to him. I had nothing else to talk about really. I knew that if I gave him a chance he would use his charm to get me right back in and continue to do the same shit.

Not this time. I meant I was leaving. I knew he would give two fucks about me being pregnant. That was another factor that played into me deciding to get the abortion.

I considered adoption. But wasn't sure if I would have been able to go through with it. Plus the kid would have enough odds against it. Both parents addicts. With a nutcase for a dad. *Fuck that too!*

Why even put that burden on somebody else if I wasn't up for it? I didn't even want anything with his DNA growing inside of me. I didn't want to have to deal with him for the rest of my life because we had a child together.

I drove up Bunny's street looking for Enoch's car. I didn't see it. I just knew Enoch's grandma was there, but then again, she may have been with one of the neighbors, shopping or something.

I parked in the driveway and walked to the door. I started feeling real funny. Butterflies and bubble guts. I guess just the thought about closing that chapter in my life made me nervous.

I walked in and headed straight toward the room that Enoch and I shared together. On my way up to the room, I saw no signs of anybody else being there. I reached for the knob on the door and was about to turn it when I heard some banging, and then moaning. It sounded like Enoch was getting his freak on.

I started to turn around, but then I decided to just go in. They could just finish the act later. I would tell the bitch she could have him. I came to get my stuff.

I was done reasoning with myself. I walked in and what I expected to see was much less disgusting than what I saw. That nigga Enoch was fucking another nigga in the ass!!!! *UGH!!! Fucking gross!!!* I wanted to hurl. I let out a loud scream then an ugh. When they heard that then they stopped.

They both jumped up and scrambled around. They tried to grab something to cover up with. I stood there in shock not only because of the fact my used to be boyfriend, would have been baby's daddy was fucking another nigga. A cute one at that.

But also the fact that the nigga he was fucking is who he copped his dope from. *What the fuck!?* That shit was sickening. As many times, as he went to meet this nigga Dre and re up! I would have never suspected that when it took a long time these niggas were getting one off! With each other!

I was always getting into it with bitches and this dude is fucking niggas. This was some Jerry Springer shit for real. A down low brother. I just shook my damn head.

Dre couldn't even look at me. He just got his shit and walked out of the room. Why was everything a lie with Enoch? He was really a stranger to me. Yeah, it was fucked up he was cheating on me with dudes and chicks.

I didn't even know he liked men. How long had that been going on? Like, was that the reason he had issues is because he was struggling with his sexuality?

He had to have a problem because he could be honest about nothing. I knew at times he couldn't tell his damn self if he was being honest or not. He did it so much and so well that it was normal. It was him. Either way, continuously lying about everything is not okay at all.

How can your mate trust you? Especially the way we rolled and the shit we did. Yet another confirmation that I needed to bounce. I didn't have time to go down for some shit he snitched on me about.

I hadn't said a word to Enoch and he hadn't said anything to me. I started putting my stuff in the trash bags that I pulled out of my purse. I turned to him and said, "I'm pregnant, it's yours but I am not keeping it." I was looking him straight in the eye. As he looked at me speechless, all I could see in his eyes was pure hatred.

But, why did he feel that way toward me? Because I caught him fuckin a dude? Was it because I was leaving? Could it have been the fact that I was killing his baby? Maybe all of the above? Did he really hate himself? Hell did he even know why he was so mad? This dude was a nut case for real.

"Bitch I'm a kill you!" he yelled out so loud that I froze. He grabbed me around my neck with one hand and started punching me in the head and face with the other. It was nothing for him to handle me that way. He was ranting and raving to the top of his lungs. He was in such a rage he, was foaming at the mouth.

He yelled right in my face, "You fuckin hoe! You just had to walk yo happy ass in this room today and see this shit didn't you? You stupid bitch!" He kept yelling! "You bet not say shit to nobody about what the fuck you just seen... you hear me?"

He punched in between rants like yo momma did when you got a whooping. It was crazy because I couldn't even fight him back. I had no energy. With the fetus that was growing inside of me and the dope habit I was trying to kick, I had nothing left.

He let go of my neck and I fell to the floor. The same floor I was laying on in a similar situation not long ago. The same floor he walked out and left me on. I had no business on that floor like that again.

He kicked me over and over again in my stomach as I laid on the floor. He kicked me with all his might. Hard as hell. He must have touched every part of my lower abdomen. He kicked me so much and so hard that I started to feel these sharp pains in my side, back, and stomach.

He grabbed me by my shirt and threw me on the bed. He climbed on top of me. He hit me constantly in my face. It felt like hot metal every time he connected his fist to my face. I had to get loose from this man before he killed me. I moved my head from side to side, trying to avoid the impact.

I don't know where the strength came from at the time and it took everything out of me to muster up enough strength to fight back. But, I found it. I hit, bit, and scratched. I did everything I could to defend myself. *Get this nigga up off of you! He is going to kill you bitch! He gone kill yo ass!*

Enoch used all his weight and strength to get my hands above my head. He began to kiss me all over my face. He was mumbling he hates me. And he doesn't give a fuck about a baby. He kissed me more and then says he loves me.

I wanted to cry but I had to break away from this man. I couldn't scream. It was like my voice was gone or my vocal cords were cut. Who would have heard me anyway?

He tried to spread my legs with his legs while he kissed my face more. I knew he was going to take the pussy. Enoch didn't take no from me. He said my pussy was his so, he would take it when he wanted it.

He didn't give a fuck about how I felt and after a while I started to think I was wrong for saying no because I was his woman. I said no so I caused him to take it.

Enoch got even more pissed off because I wouldn't let up. I was not about to just let him take me out. Out of the corner of my eye I saw the lamp. It wasn't in reach. I had to use a weapon of some sort.

It seemed like my little' taps didn't even affect him. I took a deep breath, yanked my wrist from his grasp and hit him as hard as I could right in the eye. It was a good connect. He paused for a brief second. That was all I needed.

I managed to ease over toward the little' vanity table just enough to grab the cord of the lamp. When I got the base in my grip I swung it and hit that nigga right in his head.

Then again. Then another time. I did it until I started to see red. His body fell to the side of mines and I still didn't stop. I was furious at that nigga. I was in a rage. *How you gon' put me through hell and hot water then want to beat my ass when once again you are in the wrong and got caught. Fuck you bastard!*

I didn't stop until my pain started to kick in again. I snapped out of it. I shoved his body on to the floor. I got up out of the bed and stood over him. The first thing I did was kneel down to check if he was still breathing. He was.

I felt a sense of relief yet anger and frustration all at once. I should have just finish him. Knock him off and be done with his bitch ass. As I stood back up I noticed I had blood running down my face and it was all over my hands and legs. The pain came back even sharper in my abdomen.

I had to do one last thing before I left. I did a quick spin around the room. The pain was not letting up. I knew I needed to get to the hospital and fast but I was about to pass this opportunity up. I really fought through the pain when I saw two black bags on the bed. Money and dope. I knew it had to be there because Dre was the plug.

I grabbed both bags and made my way through the door. I looked at Enoch one last time and almost started feeling sorry for him again. But I continued on my way when the pain started and reminded me I was in that fucked up position yet again because of him.

Chapter Six

I was having a miscarriage. I was cramping and having pain in my stomach. It was almost unbearable. I glanced at myself in the rear view mirror. I was beat up bad. I looked like Angela **Bassett in What's Love Got to Do With It**.

I was in pain all over, even my hands were killing me. I parked and walked into the emergency room. I was completely drained. I took one look at the triage nurse and she immediately put me a wheelchair and wheeled me back to a room. The pain was worse.

I briefed her on the way back. I told her that I was a few months pregnant and I had been fighting my, would have been baby daddy, which was my ex-boyfriend. I told her that I was in a lot of pain. Extreme pain and I was having difficulty breathing.

When I got to the room two other nurses came in to help me get changed into a gown and get cleaned up. One of them brought me Tylenol to ease some of the pain after the doctor finally came in after what seemed like hours.

He did a once over with a resident. I was pretty messed up. They told me that I had to have a pelvic exam, x-rays, and an ultrasound. They put me on oxygen because it was so painful to even breathe and if felt like I wasn't getting any air when I did.

Damn! Damn! Damn! I was at the hospital forever. I had to stay for three days. I had to get stitches in my cheek, head, and hand. I had fractured ribs, two black eyes, and a punctured lung. I didn't even notice that I was that fucked up. I also had to have a DNC.

I lost the baby. I was so out of it they gave me antidepressants. I went through withdrawals. Cold turkey. They gave some drug that was supposed to help with the cravings, but that shit did nothing.

I didn't know if I was in pain because of my injuries or because of coming off the dope. Even though I fought his ass back I knew Enoch wasn't as bad off as I was.

I was a straight basket case and I had no one to call but Kelly. I called her over a thousand times. When I didn't get an answer I left her message after message.

She never called me back. What was up with that? I called Sis, but she was nowhere to be found, either. But, just in case somebody wanted to check on me or even see where I was, I had my phone on vibrate in the bed next to me.

It was about two in the morning and I wasn't even close to going to sleep. I couldn't sleep in that hospital. I had too much on my mind. I flipped through the channels as I thought about shit and how fucked up it all was. I found some nature stuff on.

Just as I laid the remote back down on the bed my cell phone vibrated. It read: Private Caller. I knew who it was without a doubt. Enoch wanted what I had taken from his ass. His money and his dope.

It didn't matter that I was the one who had risked my life to get the shit, too. He felt like he had to be in control of it all. He gave me allowance. He wanted me to account for everything I spent it on.

He bought me other things and I used to have a part time gig for my own little change. Yet he was just down right controlling. It wasn't like that when I meet him.

He wasn't strung out either. I don't know what the hell happened, but one day he just came home doing the shit. I didn't know if he had been using the shit all along or what. But, I did know that the shit changed him. I didn't know what went on with him.

Either way, I wasn't answering that phone. I didn't wanna hear the threats and the screaming or none of that. It was pointless. He wasn't going to ask how I was.

He wasn't going to ask if I needed anything. He wasn't going to apologize. All Enoch wanted was the dope and money that I had taken from him. I'm sure he was pissed about the fact he got his ass whooped. All that made me think of how I would deal with detoxing and withdrawals. All the while having a shit load of it in my car. I knew I couldn't keep it. I had to get rid of it.

I would be right back using again if I didn't. I had already been clean for the days that I had been in the hospital and I planned to continue once I was released. Those first few days were not the worst I would face, trying to stay clean.

Could I even stay clean? I felt really bad at that moment. I felt bad for losing my baby. I felt bad for using drugs. I felt bad for beating Enoch up. I felt bad for my life. It was shitty and I didn't know what the hell to do to make it not so shitty. Between the cravings, being hungry, the hormones, and emotions; I was a complete mess.

I began to cry. I sobbed because I was hurt, damaged, and bruised. Not only my body, but my heart and my soul. I was so fed up and tired of my life that I felt like just giving up. Why live any longer? Why even try and fix the bullshit?

I really started to feel sorry for myself. I started to feel even more empty and sad. Maybe I had always felt that way inside. Maybe that was why I chose to live the way I did and put up with the bullshit from Enoch.

Could that be the answer to all of that? Or was it because I grew up thinking the only way to a man's heart was your pussy. Was it because I thought that if a man beat you that showed you his love for you.

I had plenty of irrational beliefs and at the time I didn't know or understand why? I didn't know why I felt the way I did and I couldn't remember when it started, but what I did know was that I had to change. I had to. I had to get my life on the right track.

I was okay for the most part after being released from the hospital. I had pretty much healed from the injuries. I had been staying at Sis' house since I got out. It was koo but I wanted so much to have my own spot.

I had been sharing Kelly's room with her, but she had been MIA ever since she met this dude Gerald. Only sending text messages so that we would know she was okay. But, when I thought about it, a text message didn't tell you a whole lot because anybody can send a text.

I didn't think anything of it at first though because it was sort of expected when you meet a guy and y'all digging each other, to be gone and with him all the time. As long as I knew she was okay I didn't trip.

I was trying to hold it together, but I needed to talk and vent. I needed to get this shit off my chest. I broke down. I couldn't hold it in anymore. I finally let it all out when I got to my car. I was crying, screaming, and hitting the steering wheel. I did that for at least five or six minutes.

I finally pulled myself together. I had to figure out what I would do next. My phone rang. I answered it and didn't even look at who called.

"Yeah!" I could barely get out between the cries.

"Karter!" It was Enoch 's crazy ass. I hung up the phone. I have nothing to say to him. But, that didn't stop him from calling me. He was blowing my phone up.

He called me from other numbers and even anonymous. I knew he was pissed about the money and dope I took the day I left his ass unconscious, but fuck him he would get over it.

Just the thought of him being an undercover brother just made my stomach turn. When I thought about all the shit I had done for him I was even more upset. When I remembered what all I had been through with him I knew that if I even thought about going back to him, all the shit would have only gotten worse.

I wiped my face of my tears. I knew I couldn't keep staying with Kelly and sis either. They only had a two-bedroom apartment. I knew what I had to do, but I was just so scared to be by myself. It was like I was used to a nigga taking care of me. That shit was old and so was I.

As I pulled into the gas station parking lot, my phone rang again. This time it was Kelly.

"Damn bitch, da dick dat good? Long time, no hear!" I said to her not even saying hello.

"Hey to you too hoe! What it do? And yes the dick is that good!" she said back to me. We both just fell out laughing. That was my girl for real. She was for the most part all I had aside from sis.

The rest of my family was fucked up. My mother was fighting her own demons and she sort of abandoned me at really a young age. On top of the fact I hadn't seen that lady in years. I probably wouldn't even recognize her if I did. I wasn't sure if I had siblings or not by my father but I was the only child my mother had.

I let Kelly know all about Enoch. I told her not to say anything about the down low shit. That shit was disgusting and embarrassing. I wanted the whole world to find out on their own and when I was really far out of the picture.

Not that it mattered what people thought, but you are a reflection of your mate and vice versa. You are the company you keep. The proof was in the pudding. She put that on everything that she wouldn't say a word.

I quickly changed the subject. I was tired of talking about his ass. We talked for a minute. I was almost to the apartment and we were still on the phone. She filled me in on what she and Gerald had been up to. That was her new boo and they were kicking it real heavy.

I hadn't really seen her since she meet him. I didn't know where she was some of the time. That wasn't how we rolled normally. We were close. We told each other everything. She was my cousin, but my only friend. We had been close since we were kids.

"B I T C H, you will never guess where I am!" Kelly screams in the phone. She got really hyped all of a sudden.

"Where tramp?" I said back to her. "Just guess girl!" she replies.

"Okay the mall, swimming?! What I don't know, humor me." I said back to her.

"I'm in C-A-L-I B-I-T-C-H! We doin' it real big! We poppin tags and collars! Ha!"

She was excited as hell. You could hear it all in her voice. I was happy that she was happy, but something didn't feel right. I really couldn't put my finger on it though.

Maybe it was just all the bullshit that I had gone through that made me feel that way. She went on to tell me that he was digging her for real and they went to California so that they could get away.

She said he was real cool and she didn't have to pay for anything. She told me that she thought he was a pimp and when she asked him he said no. I asked her what made her think that about him.

"Girl because he got that cake and all he ever go meet is bitches." She said.

"Where in KC or Cali?" I asked.

"Shit both. I mean they don't look like whores so maybe it's some type of escort service or something," she said.

"Well whatever it is I need you to be careful and take care of you. And please, don't let that nigga turn you out. Okay!? You is too young and too damn pretty for that shit," I told her.

"Girl, I'm good! That nigga ain't like that. He ain't gone turn me out. I ain't no weak bitch anyway," she said.

You don't even know him, is what I thought, but I kept it to myself. It was not the time for that. I just knew that I would hate for that nigga Gerald to have my girl all the way the fuck in Cali out there bad like that. I knew the shit women did shit for money. Period.

Fuck I did, but I didn't let a nigga pimp me. I didn't let a man use me to get money by making me do whatever sexually to a person.
Only to go and give all the money just made back to the nigga that's making me do it.

Wait, Karter, I thought to myself. That sounds just like me and Enoch. At that moment, I came to an epiphany. Right then I understood just what she went through. I was doing the same thing with Enoch. But, what I had to do first was deal with my own situation before I could even think about hers. I had to find my own place and a job.
A good one. I didn't want to be another statistic. I didn't want to end up like everybody around me. Fucked up, broke, and pissed at the world cause they old, still chasing a high or drink, and still ain't got shit.

But my problem was I loved money and all the shit it brought. I loved to dress cute in the latest and most expensive.

I had all the new shoes, purses and cloths. I had jewelry as well. I kept a good nice wig or nice hair do. And it was nothing to drop some cash and get right in the club.

I loved being able to cut the line at the clubs. I enjoyed the attention and how people noticed you when you had money. I wanted the bottles and the VIP service at the clubs.

I liked that type of shit. I liked it all. I liked it so much I had done some shit to make sure I was able to keep getting and doing it. That was one of the reasons I was in the position I was in. Running and addicted.

Chapter Seven

I was on my hustle. I had to get rid of that dope and fast. I called one of my cousins. She was in the game heavy. I knew she would cop all of the dope as long as the price was right. I was for sure going to make her an offer she couldn't refuse.

One person to dump it all to was perfect for me. I didn't have time to try and nickel and dime the dope. Shit I didn't have time to try and keep reinvesting and flipping and doubling.

I didn't have time for none of that shit. When it was time for me to move and get my shit in order, I needed to have cash on deck, or at least access to it.

I rode around to see a few apartments that I had found in the apartment guide that was at the newsstand. I went to these lofts and they looked cool from the outside. The location was sort of midtown near the plaza.

The plaza was a pretty upscale part of the city. It was the heart of good ole KC! Other parts of the city weren't all that, just like the raggedy ass lofts I saw. That was why the fuck they were so damn cheap. I was NOT about to stay there. Close to the plaza or not, it was a dump! So on to the next one.

I went to like four apartments and only one I liked. It was all utilities paid and it included a full size washer and dryer. That part really didn't matter because I didn't wash anything, but underwear. I took most of my wardrobe to the cleaners.

The thing was the rent was higher which only made sense because that was all I paid. It was centrally located right off the highway. They were new and they were running a special. NO DEPOSIT.

I got the application filled it out, got a money order for the application fee, and took it right back. I couldn't let that pass me by. The fact that I would be in my own place in about month didn't make me happy.

You would think a person would be super amped about moving into their own spot soon. Not me. I mean I was glad, but that's it. It may have been because it hadn't hit me yet. With the state of mind I was in, it would have taken a lot to get me happy.

I wanted to go home and lay down, but I knew that wouldn't help. I was down and out, and sleep would have just added to the already dark feelings I was having.

I didn't want to take my life or have my life taken, but I almost felt like it was the only solution. I could escape everything I was dealing with. I wouldn't be here to deal with any of it. People said that suicide was selfish, but fuck I didn't have kids. I didn't have a husband.

My deadbeat ass mother wasn't even around. The doctors told me to keep taking my antidepressants and to resume normal activity, but not to go too hard.

I wanted to just curl up and fucking die. But, instead I made my way to the L I Q for a good ole cigarillo. I had a stash at the house. I was used to smoking with Kelly, but my dawg hadn't been home for a min so I had been taking them to the face by myself.

That day I came into Kelly and Sis' house full of a mutha fucka's. Kelly's' sister wasn't always there, but when she was she kept it cracking. Smoking, drinking, dominos, cards, hair braiding, food the whole nine.

Hell you might find somebody getting they freak on if some pills had been popped! Her name was Keisha, but we called her SIS. She was cool, but sometimes she made you want to just stick her ass. She has a slick ass mouth on her.

"Hey y'all," I said as I walked in the apartment. It wasn't as packed as it usually was. Just a handful of people. Some spoke and some didn't. I just headed back to my room. When I got in the room that Kelly and I shared I put my stuff on the bed and put my purse up.

I kept it and everything else of major importance to me hidden. Out of sight. You never knew who you could trust. I got my weed out, sat on the bed, and twisted up. I was done in no time flat. I lit it up and boy was it fire.

It was some of dat ooh wee I got from my plug. I haven't used any dope since I left the hospital, but boy did I crave it something terrible. I was upfront and honest with the doctors when I was there. They told me I may have the cravings forever. I was like what the fuck?

They said that's the way that drug affected you. It was that powerful. I was surprised that I was even able to stop it. The way I was strung out, I didn't even have hope in myself that I would be able to quit. I just hoped and prayed I could continue to be more powerful than the cravings.

I had allowed Enoch to turn my life upside down. I let him control me and use me at his leisure. What's crazy was the mind games he played. He always thought that I shouldn't smoke, but laced my shit with Coke and made me smoke it.

Would shake me out a few lines to snort in a heartbeat. That was some crazy shit! Just the thought of his dick in some niggas ass made me sick to my stomach.

I sat there deep in my thoughts as I smoked almost half of the blunt. I decided to finish the rest with the peeps in the front room. I would just sit back and laugh at they ass. They were some characters. I walked to the living room and found me a piece of a spot on the couch. It wasn't a lot of places to sit to start with.

It was only one couch and a card table with four chairs. One recliner and a fuckin bean bag.
   A place to sit was few and far between in that joint. After I got settled into my small spot on the couch I took another puff of the blunt and passed it. I just sat on the couch stuck, laughing, and bullshiting with everybody.

   I listened to them and what they talked about. It was shit that didn't even matter. Things like this person or that person. Who had and was doing what with who.

   I didn't want to always be the one that was talking about people. I wanted to be the one that everybody was talking about, but in a different way. At least not with the shit my name was usually associated with.

   When my name would come up it would be in mess and associated with one of the many fucked up things I did for or with Enoch. Who they thought we robbed. Who I was supposed to had set up. Who they thought I was fucking and all that. O and let's not forget all the bitches and shit behind Enoch. They kept my name in their mouths.

   I was used to hearing the shit, but then I thought why was I mad. Why was I upset the people were talking about me and the shit I did. I knew I needed to let some things from my past go, to be able to move forward with my life, but fuck that.

Knock! Knock! Knock! Somebody was banging like the police. Took me all out of my element. I jumped up to answer the door, but then thought twice about it. Too much shit had been going on lately and that could have been anybody behind that door.

I turned and looked at Sis. She gave me a head shake and a certain look that said don't answer the door and get somewhere other than that front room. I immediately found a place to hide. It wasn't the best spot, but whoever was at that door wasn't about to find me.

I only knew that because the spot was in the kitchen. The way the apartment was setup you had to go through the front room to get there. That wasn't about to happen because whoever it was would have had to have gone past Sis.

Once I was out of sight I tried to keep calm and listen to who it was and what went on.

"WHO IS IT?" Sis shouted.

"IT'S Enoch!" he replied.

The banging started again. My heart instantly went to my stomach when I heard his voice. That spooked the hell out of me. I almost peed my pants. I knew that I would have to face Enoch one day, but I didn't want it to be that soon and I for damn sure didn't think it was going to be like that.

Sis opens the door a little to talk to him, but instead he just pushed the door open and brushes past her. Once he was in the house he instantly went to the bedrooms to look for me. I could hear almost everything from the hiding spot. From what I heard shit was about to get real.

"Enoch, if you don't stop going through my house like that we gone have a mutha fuckin' problem! Who the fuck you think you are? Didn't nobody even invite you in this bitch!" Sis said to him. She was pissed and I didn't blame her.

"You need to check yo' self, Enoch, and leave now for shit get ugly!" she pleaded with him one last time.

"Aw yeah. So, it's like that, Sis? You lying for her now? That bitch is here I know she is," He said. He walked by her yet another time. He was even more pissed by then because he didn't find anything or me.

"Pussy, get the fuck out of my house! I told you she ain't here and you goes through my shit anyway like I'm a liar! Now, I'm a say this for the last time! GET THE FUCK OUT!" Sis said to Enoch.

"I ain't going nowhere, BITCH!!! And yo bitch ass cousin stole from me!" he yelled back. He was beside himself. What he didn't see was all them niggas in the house, and they were all packing.

"I bet I don't leave until somebody comes up with my goddamn shit!!!" he says. "Bet I don't. On the mutha fuckin set I don't leave!"

The nigga Enoch was bugging. By that time every nigga in the house was to they feet. Guns drawn or about to be. One cat had his gun in hand with his finger on the trigger.

They were ready. Enoch was still talking shit. "I'm a kill that punk bitch when I see her hoe ass!" "She got me fucked up!" "Don't NOBODY take shit from Enoch!" he was yelling and getting amped even more.

"Enoch, just leave. SHE AINT HERE!!" Sis said to him one more time. "Go home and call her. Hell, go look for her somewhere else just get the fuck out of here!" Sis knew what it was.

See the dude that was half braided, no shirt on, with his finger on the trigger was Jay, sis's man. Ever since I could remember he had been around. They had that break up to make up shit. Can't live without each other type of relationship. The funny thing to me was that they had no kids, together or outside of the relationship.

That was because they knew the other one would kill they ass. Jay had a few screws loose. He was cool as a fan and laid back, too, but if you fuck with Sis it was O V. Done deal buddy. He didn't play when it came to her. The other three dudes with him, lets just say birds of a feather flock together. They were his niggas ride or die like.

"Hey, playboy! The lady of the house told you to raise up. I'm a need fa you to respect that and bounce! My NIGGA!" He said to Enoch calm, but sternly despite his aggressive behavior. Jay was right in the nigga face. He stayed ready.

I knew for damn sure Enoch was high and most likely out of his mind. No telling how many days he had been up or what all he had been taking. Either way, Enoch knew how Jay got down. He knew what type of nigga Jay was just like Jay knew what type of nigga Enoch was.

Enoch was low key scared of Jay. He was one of them niggas that the whole city knew and didn't fuck with because he didn't play any games. He was the type of nigga that handled his shit and took care of business. Period. He was a solid nigga. But again he didn't fuck around when it came to Sis.

A few years back there was a time where Sis and Jay were off. They both started talking to other people. The guy that Sis was seeing started acting crazy and stalking and shit when Sis wasn't feeling him any longer. She told Jay about it. He waited outside until the nigga came one night to sit and stalk her. Not sure what happened, but she never seen or heard from him again. Nobody did.

"Jay, fuck you! You think 'because you got that piece you bitch ass nigga I'm supposed to bitch up and run like a little punk. Ha yeah okay. I'm a stay right here until she shows the fuck up. What you gonna shoot me!? Huh nigga?! Yo bitch ass ain't gone do shit!" Enoch said.

Every cat in that house surrounded him. Jay put the safety on and put his gun in his back. Then he let one loose on his ass! He hit him right in his nose hard as a mutha fucka!!!! Blood just instantly start gushing out.

He must have broken his shit! All the other dudes joined in and whooped his ass!!! I knew Enoch was mad about his dope and money, but I didn't think he would go there with Jay!!! He was just too far out of his mind that he didn't care what happened, to him or anybody else. They had to literally drag him out. They beat him unconscious.

I have no idea where they took him, but they did it quick. I just knew they would kill him, but I guess they didn't because it was my ex-boyfriend. He had done a little' business with him before and Sis and I were cousins. So for the most part they had been cool and cordial in the past.

Chapter Eight

I knew that I had to get the fuck outta dodge. That nigga Enoch was not about to let me get away with that money and dope like that. He was molly whopped by Jay so I'm sure I'm the blame for that too. Either way I had to go.

But where? I needed my own place. That was a fact. At the same time where could I hide out from Enoch at in the city? He knew it inside out and he knew most of the people in it. It would only be a matter of time before he would find me. I was sure of it.

I was spooked for days after that incident. I immediately started freaking out. My mind went to the dope. I wanted a hit. I needed a snort. I had to have a line. I was tripping out.

I had to gather my thoughts and chill. I sure the fuck didn't need to start using again. I had to relax and figure this shit out. So for the next few days to follow I got a room near the airport. I needed to make sure I thought things through.

I knew I could no longer even go over Sis's and I sure as hell knew that staying in the city was not an option, either. It was at the point where I knew I had to leave.

If I didn't no telling what would end up happening. I couldn't deal with that, either. I would have to kill Enoch. Straight like that. I knew he was pissed and I knew he was going to come after me and I also knew that nigga was capable of anything and would stop at nothing.

I had just gotten the money for the dope I sold to my cousin. She bought all of it like I thought she would. It was two kilos to be exact. I sold them for 20,000 apiece.

She was happy to pay that amount. She said she had been getting them for no less than 27,500. But on the street they can go for 30,000. I just needed the cash and fast to get the fuck away.

I was changing my life and I needed that money to do so. I had gotten about 15,000 from Enoch when I took the dope. I was set. That would allow me to move however I wanted to. I had a slight dilemma because how the fuck was I going to get on the plane with all that cash like that? Fuck it. I would have to drive the Mero.

I wrapped with my cousin and told her all of the shit that was going on. I told her how Enoch was on my heels and that I had to get the fuck outta town. I told her I was thinking about, Atlanta.

I had always wanted to visit there. Everybody always said that black folks were living good and doing it big down there. I wanted a change. I needed that. I figure the only way for me to stay clean, safe, and out of the way, was to get the fuck away from Kansas City.

I repacked my car with everything I had taken out of it and into the hotel room. I was ready to bounce. I had enough time to clear my head. I had enough time to process my life and the last few recent events.

I knew I had created an even bigger mess for myself by taking Enoch's money and dope, but part of that shit was mine. I was not about to walk away broke and looking stupid. I already felt dumb as hell and he beat my ass good on top of that, made me lose my child.

But, I felt like FUCK Enoch!! He could kiss my entire ass. I was nervous, but I felt good. I felt like I was on my way to liberation. I had my game plan and I was ready to execute.

When I first got to Atlanta I stayed in a hotel room for a few nights. After I talked to my cousin who copped the dope from me, I was connected with one of her close home girls. Her name was Anita and she took me right under her wing and helped me get all the way on my feet. Like big boy status. Bossy!

She was already there so who better to teach you. She used to be in the game just like my cousin was, but got out after two of her kids got killed and she went to jail for 5 years. Dope deal gone bad. It was tragic, but she turned her life around once she got out. She chose Atlanta as the city to start over in. She fucking bubbled.

See everybody in Atlanta is into beauty and fashion. On top of the high population of successful black people. Anita owned several beauty salons, hair supply stores, and a chain of cosmetology schools. Not to mention the real estate and construction companies. She had it going on.

She began to show me the ropes, told me what do, and how to make my money work for me. She told me to always have something to fall back on, some type of trade. She used to do hair on the street and in prison. When she got out she used that as a stepping stone to work her way up. She made it.

I had the cash that I stole from Enoch and from selling the dope. I was GOOD. I wanted to do something legit with my money and I wanted to make sure I invested it well.

I wanted to own shit and be able to take trips for weeks and months at a time out of country. I wanted to have a chef. I wanted to not only dress nice and get VIP. I wanted to own the building the VIP was in. I thought big. I had no choice. I wanted lived the glamorous life.

The first step was to go to hair school to get my license. I enrolled in Anita's hair school and took classes immediately. I stayed with her for a short time. While I was there it was like I stayed alone in a big ass house.

The maid would stop through 3 times a week and the chef as well. I didn't know anybody so I didn't have company. I only went out to eat and shop. I loved living in Atlanta after I was only there for a month. I knew I would have to get a place of my own. Although, it was gravy staying there I couldn't wear out my welcome and I wanted my OWN space.

One day as I was exploring the city and looking to find a nice area to live in, I got a phone call. It was Sis.

"Yes." I answered.

"Karter!!!" Sis cried hysterically.

"What is wrong, Sis? Where are you? You okay?" I asked in one breath.

"No!" And she began to cry again.

"What happened?" I asked her.

"I'm at Truman." She managed to get out between cries. "Jay just got shot and he in surgery." She cried more.

I couldn't believe what I heard. I didn't even know what to say. She was a damn mess and I could hear it in her voice. She kept talking, telling me the story, or what she could get out between tears. She couldn't even catch her breath because she cried so hard. She finally was able to talk.

She started to tell me, but couldn't finish because Jay's people started coming in greeting her one by one. He had a very large family and everybody from the momma and her people to all the friends of the family showed up.

The family of the other people he was with started to come, too. He was shot as well. His cousin Mustafah, his ace boom, was in life threatening condition and they didn't think he would make it. His boy, Mike, had already died.

This shit was crazy. Everybody was crying, pissed off, cursing, or screaming. I could hear them. Sis didn't want me to hang up so I didn't. It was so many emotions flying in that hospital.

Eventually they moved them to their own room for family members. I had to smoke and quick. I grabbed the blunt out of the ashtray and lit it up. I wanted to get lifted to the fucking clouds. I inhaled the blunt and we began to chat some more.

"Have you talked to Kelly?" she asked me first.

"No have you?" I asked.

"No, but that nigga got her on some bull shit for real!!! I been taking care of us since our mom died. We have never gone this long without talking. Even if we were into it," She said.

I could hear the pain in her voice. She started to cry again, but managed to say. "My sister gone now and my man may be too! What am I going to do, Karter?" "I'm so fucked up right now." She said to me.

"Listen to me." I told her, "He gonna make it! And Kelly is still your sister. I am sure she will be back soon. Watch what I say. Now what in the hell happened? Who did this shit to Jay?"

"Ya boy, Enoch! I couldn't believe the shit, either. Jay was leaving the 7-11 on Linwood and Enoch was coming. They bumped heads in the parking lot. Enoch drew his gun first. It was just him and one other cat. They had a shootout right there." She said barely able to get it all out without crying again.

What the fuck!? Enoch signed his death certificate. He sealed the deal for himself. He was out of control and that was the second person that I would have never expected him to harm or attempt to kill. It was even more clear to me that Enoch had lost his mind and he was headed for straight destruction.

He was on a rampage. He had a death wish. He was determined to sabotage any and everything that he felt was against him or that he felt threatened by. Enoch wanted everyone to feel pain because he seemed to be in so much of it. Just like I was. In pain.

"The other dude Robert died right there on the scene. Enoch is at KU hospital. At first, they were trying to charge Jay with murder, but they don't even know, which bullets killed who yet." She started to cry again. "I just pray Jay don't die."

"It will be okay, sweetie." I told her as I wished I was there to comfort her. "He is a fighter."

"I know, Karter. This is all just fucked up, but I love you girl," she said.

"I love you, too, Sis." I said.

I hung the phone up and finished the blunt. I didn't even feel like continuing on my search. I was fucked up. My heart and mind were heavy as hell. I felt so bad. I felt responsible for the man being in that condition. If I would have just answered the door that day. I should have just opened and dealt with Enoch myself.

I put somebody else in my bullshit. I put an innocent person in harm's way yet again. I shouldn't have even took the money and dope. I was mad at myself. I was pissed at Enoch punk ass, too.

I saw right then that if he didn't die I was gone have to kill that nigga myself. He would stop at nothing. He didn't care what he had to do, but he would get me. That was crystal clear.

I felt a slight sense of relief when Kelly called me back after the doctors told her that Jay pulled through surgery and was in ICU. He was not all the way in the clear, but his chances were good. Sis sounded so much better once she heard that. She felt like she had some hope.

I didn't know how to feel about Enoch in the hospital possibly dying. On one hand I was happy that I didn't have to deal with his bitch ass anymore and on the other I wanted to go and see him and be with him.

Yet that nigga just tried to murk my people. I was sure it would be me if he would have gotten the chance. Once again I was worried and thinking about that scandalous as nigga and he was out to kill me!!

I kept thinking if I would have never even taken the money and dope then Enoch wouldn't have been after me. I should have just gone outside and faced my own fire that day.

There it was my cousins man in the hospital in critical condition because of choices I made. I did not at all like the feeling that I felt knowing that. That shit was started to get too close to the people I loved and cared about.

The shit I did in the streets shouldn't come back to the people around me. I guess this was a little different because I considered Enoch my family at one point so that's who I brought him around, my family.

Who knew that we would be in that situation? Who knew Enoch would have tried to kill Jay for some shit I had done and was trying to run from.

Chapter Nine

I got on the first flight out of Atlanta to KC. I had to get there to check on Sis and see what the fuck would happened with Enoch. I landed, got me a rental, and went straight to the hospital where she was. She was happy to see me and I was damn sure happy to see her. We talk for a while, and then I was able to visit with Jay also. He was still in ICU so I couldn't stay long. She told me she would be home later.

I let her know I would get a room. I was not about to stay in her house. No telling who was looking at who came and went. I got a room at the Marriott on the plaza. I unloaded the car, took a bath, and tried to go to sleep.

I finally was able to drift off. I had so much on my mind it was pitiful. Just being in that city made my stomach knot up. It was like the whole city had bad energy or was that because I normally put bad energy out there, so that's what the hell I got back. I knew I wouldn't stay there long.

The next day I was up at 6 a.m. I had to make it to the African's shop to get my hair braided. I was supposed to get it braided in ATL that same day. I was fried by the head and needed to do something with it.

I could have whipped it up myself but I needed a break. I got to the shop and sat in the car until the first hair braider came and unlocked the door. I walked in about five minutes later and she was ready for me. She started right then.

A few more people came and before you knew it the shop was packed. This particular time was no different than any other time I had been in that shop to get my hair braided.

I sat there and tried not to focus on the pain by channeling my attention on other things around me. I tried not to be nosey but it was hard because my phone was charging so I had nothing to do. This chick in the other chair next to me was talking to another girl. The friend was sitting in a chair close to her, waiting to get serviced. However, they were chopping it up.

They were talking about everybody in the city. This one topic really stood out. It had all of my attention. They discussed Enoch having HIV. *What in the hell!?* I thought. *I must be hearing shit!* I thought I was tripping. I thought it must be another Enoch, but when the chick said the girl's name I had the fight with I knew it was Enoch.

I couldn't wait until she was finished. Time seemed to go really slow after that. All types of things came to my mind. I could hardly sit there until she was done.

I wanted to ask the two girls that was talking to give me more information but how much did they really know? Plus, I didn't want them to think I was blind to anything. Even though I had no earthly idea of any of it. I was glad they didn't seem to recognize me. I didn't have time for that drama either.

I started to text Kelly, but decided that is more like a phone call type of conversation. My hair was finally done being braided. I was about to run up out of that chair.

I paid the lady braiding me, took a good look, and I was out of the door. My hair was laid, real cute, and it was going to last me for a while.
My head was tight as hell, but I had taken an ibuprofen when she was almost done so I was good. No headache.

As soon as I got to my car the first person I called was Enoch, but his phone was disconnected. *What?* I called back same thing. My heart was beating one hundred beats a minute. I was scared as hell.

What if I had it?? O my GOSH!!!! Is the shit even true?? And why in the fuck is this niggas' phone off!? Okay Karter! Calm down. Get some facts before you get hysterical.

I called the doctor's office I went to before I left KC. They were cool as hell and was able to get me in ASAP after I explained the situation. I got to the doctor's office in less than twenty minutes.

They did a rapid test, which came back negative. I was so glad about that. But, my doctor wanted blood draws just to be cautious. I got my blood drawn in like three minutes. They told me I would have my results with in seventy-two hours.

That was too damn long, but what choice did I have but to wait. I would die of anticipation. I knew the rapid was negative, but that wasn't good enough for me either. I had been sleeping with this man with no protection for a very long time.

On top of that my doctor wanted me to start on Pre-Exposure Prophylaxis treatment. I told the doctor's office to call my cell phone as soon as they got my results back. I left the doctor's office and headed right to Bunny's house.

I called Bunny's house when I was on my way. She didn't answer. Her answering machine stated that she was out, but to leave her a message and if it was for Enoch he no longer lived there. I was on my way to their house. I made sure I had my strap loaded ready with one in the head.

I needed some damn answers and I needed them at that moment. But, I wasn't about to go over there without protection. That was for damn sure. Then I had to ask myself what was I going to say to Enoch if he was there?

Did I forget that he is after me for the money and dope I stole from him? Did I forget that he could possibly be dead from the shootout with Jay? I was con fucking fused once again behind him. It never fucking fails.

I kept driving, anyway. I wanted to see what the hell was going on. If Enoch was dead or alive, Bunny would have the entire scoop. When I got to the house it looked deserted.

Maybe nobody lived there anymore. I went to the door and rang the doorbell. No answer just like the phone. I knocked on the door for a long ass time. I just knew somebody had to be in there. Still no one came.

As I walked back to my car I saw one of the neighbors. Ms. Bertha. She had stayed on that block for years and when I say she knew everything, she knew everything.

She knew it all about everybody on the block. I had to go talk to her. I went over and asked what had happened to the people who lived in that house. She remembered exactly who I was so she didn't hold back any information. She started right in.

"Chile, Ms. Williams don't live at that there house no mo. No ma-am. That boy done sent her to have a stroke. Young as she is. She couldn't do for hu self no mo afta dat. She at a nursing home off of Swope Parkway now." She told me.

"Ms. Bertha when did all of this happen?" I asked her. "Have you seen Enoch at all?" "Not on a while. Last I knew dat boy was in jail." She said back to me "Police came by the house and picked 'em up a while back."

"Some say it was because of the drugs and other say because he got dat disease. You know, dat AIDS/HIV shit! And was still around here screwing with a dirty little dick! Just nasty!" she said with this look of disgust on her face.

"And you know he was doing men, too! Mmmmm huh! Damn shame, but if you ask me. That's right. God don't like ugly. Ms. Williams bless, her little' soul, been in there since all this mess hit the fan.

She paralyzed on one side and can't talk to well. Gotta stay in a wheelchair just ta half way get around." She finally stopped giving me the run down as she sat in her lawn chair on her porch. It was a lot to take in, but I'm glad I got some damn answers. I'm glad I know what the fuck is going on now.

"Well Ms. Bertha I got to go. But, thank you for catching me up on everything." I told her. "Okay, baby. But, you make sure you go get yo little self-checked out. Betta hope that boy didn't pass that mess to you." She said to me. "And it's a good thing you left from wit him when you did. He was liable ta kill you."

I almost broke down in tears right there on her porch. *How in the hell did she know he was beating my ass? I guess I wasn't hiding it as good as I thought.* I said to myself.

I just thanked her again for the info and headed to my car. I wondered if Enoch was still in the hospital or had they taken him into custody? *When did he find out he had HIV? And was he still calling my phone wherever he was? Trifflin' as nigga!*

He was out here fucking dudes and chicks. No telling how many contracted this disease from him. It was still amazing to me how people still didn't really understand how you got the disease, who carries it, and the whole nine.

The shit was serious and people were dying from it. Which was what happened to Sis and Kelley's mom. She contracted the disease and ended up catching the chickenpox.

Chickenpox wasn't that big of a deal, but since she was positive and her immune system was already compromised she couldn't fight them off. It spread to her brain and she died. We were still kids when it happened, so we didn't understand everything at the time.

My mother really went wild after that. Losing her sister put her over the edge. She wasn't the same since. She stayed in the streets and that became her life. I was no longer first in it.

That seemed to be the beginning of my life of hell. That seemed to be when things took a turn for the worst. Kelly, Sis, and I are so close because of it. We didn't have anybody, but each other.

Up until my mother took to the streets she had a steady boyfriend and that was the closeted thing to a father I knew. His name was Paul. He treated me like his child and tried to be there as much as he could.

But when he moved on and found himself another woman it caused problems between them. She couldn't understand why he took care of a kid that wasn't his from a woman he was no longer with and was never married to.

I heard stories of this person being my dad, that person, but I didn't know for sure. The one story that made the most sense to me was the one that came from a family friend.

She was supposedly close with my mom and her siblings growing up. The story was my father was incarcerated and had been for years. She told me my mother never told him about me because she didn't want me around the life he lived. *The way mine turned out was better?*

That seemed to be yet another thing she held on to. I wondered who the hell he was. I was sure I would find out the truth and who he really was one day. Or I wanted to believe I would.

That may had been part of the reason I was so fucked up. I didn't know who my biological father was and men in my life had always taken advantage of me.

Yeah I would say that sure plays a part. If I ever saw my mother again I would ask her who he was and why she kept it from me? *Was he that bad?*

Thinking of my mother brought up memories of my childhood and losing my aunt and all. Then I couldn't help but to wonder if I had HIV, too. I wanted my test results ASAP! I was dying to know if I was negative or not. The test I got wasn't enough for me.

Even if I was negative once the blood test came back, the doctor told me that I still needed to be tested every six months and that I also needed to use protection. All the time. I felt like the best protection would be not to have sex at all.

But what about my last trip to the hospital?
I thought. *Did they not check my status then?*
I'm sure they tested me. But do they have to
ask? Did they even ask me? It was a lot going on
that night in the hospital. And some of it I don't
remember.

Yet, I had to know and waiting for days to
get the results for my HIV test was eating at me.
It caused me to really, really wanna get high. I
wanted to escape all the bull shit.

I wanted a bump. I wanted a bump bad. I
wanted to get so fucking high that I had no
choice, but to feel numb. I wanted to forget
about those last few months of my life.

I started to get shaky and feel sick to my
stomach. I had been doing damn good since I
was released from the hospital that last time. No
coke at all. It was hard as hell, though. The
doctors didn't lie when they said I would have the
cravings. Those bitches were strong.

I didn't know how else to deal with it tho.
Getting high was my only outlet. That was the
only way I had dealt with things for so long. I
didn't know what else to do.

I had so many emotions going on with me I couldn't figure out what to do. All I could think of was where I had stashed some dope. I started to think of all the places I used to hide some from Enoch. I started to recall where the last place I had kept the dope.

Then it dawned on me, I didn't have any dope stashed. I remembered that I didn't live with Enoch and Bunny anymore. I remembered that I hadn't snorted dope in quite some time.

I remembered that I didn't even live in Kansas City anymore and I was headed back to my home. If I could just get through the next couple of days without getting high and into even more shit, I was winning.

I started to cry because I was distraught and just couldn't get my thoughts together. I was fucked up because it seemed no matter what I did I was always in some shit.

Something was always haunting me. Following me. It was like I had a black cloud over my ass and when it rained it mutha fucking poured. I began to get angry. My tears stopped and I could feel myself getting warm.

My heart was already beating fast from all the moving and emotions I was feeling. I knew I had to relax and calm down. I felt like I was having a panic attack. I couldn't catch my breath. I started to sweat and get light headed.

Why was I going to relapse over Enoch? why was this nigga still affecting me and my life? It wasn't him per say, but he was the reason that I may have had HIV/AIDS.

After I started to finally calm down I started to feel sorry for myself. I told myself that it was okay to go out and get high. I told myself that one line would be okay. I told myself that it was no big deal. I told myself I needed it.

Chapter Ten

I decided to get some dope. *Fuck it! I could be dying anyway.* I wiped my face with my hands, started my car, and I was out. I pulled off from Bunny's house with one mission and one mission only. I would roll through the hot spots, get my shit, and then back to the room to snort.

Why not? Jay was in the hospital possibly dying. I might have been dying. Why not snort some dope and get on a different level?

I started on my journey to find what it was I thought would numb me from the pain and heartache of my bullshit ass life. I was just starting to feel normal again and then all that.

I ended up on 55 and Prospect. If it wasn't a little slanger out there, it was definitely be somebody there who could point me in the right direction. But, to my surprise there wasn't a soul in sight. I kept rolling north. It had to be a hooker, crackhead, or something down that street.

I kept riding. I started to wonder what the hell I was about to do if I couldn't find any dope. I started to imagine my life strung out again. What did I look like doing somebody hair high as fuck off some coke!!! How was I going to be successful and own multiple businesses as a dope feign??

What did I look like running back to the bathroom every five mins to do a line?!?! How was I going to be professional powdering my nose!?!?! I snapped out of my daze when I almost ran the red light at 31st and Prospect.

I didn't need to keep riding, looking for dope or somebody to get me my dope. I decided to just take my ass back to the hotel room and figure out my life without the coke. I figured getting high off a blunt was actually better.

I could get on my level and still be able to think. I began to head back to the room so I could smoke until I passed out or the crazy thing that I called my life started to make sense.

I ended up turning around in this restaurant parking lot off 29th and Prospect. As I looked I saw the sign read, "Jamaican Cuisine". I thought to myself, *Lets try some*. Let me be adventurous. I had never had Jamaican food before.

I parked, made sure my heat was under the seat, and then proceeded to walk in the building. The man at the counter caught my eye immediately.

I was so instantly intrigued by him the thought of all the other bullshit had left my mind that quick. I approached the counter and he says, "Hello and welcome to Jamaican Cuisine"! In his Jamaican accent.

I just stared at him. I didn't even know what to say. The nigga was fine as hell!!! He stood about 6'3" brown skinned with dreads. It wasn't until he said, "Waah Gwan" that I was taken out of my glaze.

I snapped out of it and replied, "Excuse me." I was embarrassed because I didn't know what the hell that meant, and also because I was caught staring at him.

It was something about him that didn't allow me to take my eyes off of him. At that moment I had forgotten about wanting a bump. I had forgotten all about the fact that I could be HIV positive. This man had me mesmerized.

He smiled at me and began to translate what he meant. It was just another way of saying, "what's up". He continued to talk to me. He told me his name. It was Judah. Some of what he said I understood and other things I needed him to repeat. He asked me had I ever eaten Jamaican food before. If I had ever been to Jamaica and what type of food did I like.

There were other patrons in the restaurant as well as other people working there. He was very polite and made sure everyone was helped. We continued to converse.

I explained to him that I had never had Jamaican food and never been to Jamaica, but would go. He said he knew just the dish I should try. He turned to a fellow worker and said something to him I could not understand. He then turned back to me and said for me to come with him.

We entered the kitchen. There was a stool that he motioned for me to sit on. The people in the kitchen smiled and greeted me. I greeted them back. He then made me a small plate with chicken, rice with beans, and cabbage.

He passed me the plate, and then a fork. "Try dis ya." I did as I was told. I was a little skeptical at first. The chicken was covered with brown gravy and as I picked it with the fork it just fell off the bone. I took a piece and I ate it. It was good. It was seasoned just right and the meat was tender. I must have made some type of face when I ate be it because Judah started to smile.

I liked food just as much as the next person, but that chicken that he had me taste, was the best I had eaten in a long time. I finished all of what was on my plate. As I did so, we sat and talked more.

He told me that he was born in Jamaica and that he had been in the states for years now. We didn't get into too much personal stuff, we kept it light. I didn't want to get to know anybody in that fashion, especially since I didn't know my status at that moment in time. On top of that I didn't even live in that city anymore.

It was something about that man that had me captivated, still. I told him that I had to go and thanked him for letting me try the food. I asked him if I could place a to go order so that I could have some later. He reached for a Styrofoam container and made me a plate to go.

He bagged it and handed it to me. He motioned for me to follow him. I did so. He leads me back through the kitchen and back to the front of the restaurant, which was empty at this point.

He stopped, turned around, and just stared at me for a minute. He said something to me I couldn't understand. I asked him to repeat himself. He sort of chuckled a little, and said, "Mi waah di numba enuh?" I understood exactly what he asked at that point. He wanted the digits. I didn't know what to do.

I didn't know if I should give them to him or not. After all I didn't want to start something I couldn't finish, nor did I want anybody to contract anything from me. I had to be sure of my status.

I also had to be sure that talking to another man was something I wanted to do. But, I had to move on at some point. I knew that. I had to put all that shit behind me or at least try to. I gave him my number. He gave me his. He told me that he would call me when he got back from out of town. I didn't hold my breath.

I cried myself to sleep that night. When I woke up the next morning I hoped all the shit was a bad dream. My eyes were swollen and bloodshot red. I could barely open them.

Between the weed and all the crying. I was done. I had stayed up most of the night thinking about Enoch and the HIV situation. As well as Jay being in the hospital.

I had to find Enoch. I just couldn't stay in KC past the few days I had already planned. I knew I couldn't go to the hospital and kill him either. That was way too risky. He mostly likely was going back to jail but who knows how long. I had enough money to put a hit out for him but I didn't want anybody to know anything. I wanted this handled on my own.

My pounding head took me out of my plot to find Enoch and take him out. The cravings for the coke were still there, strong and in full effect. I promised myself that I was not going to give into them.

I laid there trying to get the strength to get up and do something with myself. I was really ready to go back to Atlanta. This damn city just kept me in a funk. I didn't have not one craving when I was in ATL. I was back in Kansas City and it all hits me like a fucking brick.

My phone rang and I was in such a mood I just answered with, "What?!"

"What? Bitch, what the fuck is the deal hoe? What it do?" It was Kelly.

"Kelly?!" I said. I knew her voice, but she sounded different, but then again maybe it was me.

"Well I'll be damned! Long time no hear! I thought you forgot about ya girl. How are you and where in the hell are you?" I asked.

"I'm still in Cali! I'm just sitting here on the balcony, smoking a square, enjoying the weather," she said.

"Well I wish I could say the same. I'm laying here just crying my eyes out. I just found out Enoch got HIV. At this point I am not sure if he is even still alive or not." I said.

"What in the hell!? That nigga was out there bad for real! Have you gotten tested?" She asked me.

"Yeah I went yesterday when I found out. The rapid was negative, but I haven't gotten my results back yet from the blood draw. This shit is so crazy I want to scream!" I told her.

"Girl and I thought I had drama. How about I haven't seen Gerald in about a week! And I think I am pregnant," she said.

"Okay bitch, it's either you are or you ain't. You know if you knocked up or not. When are you coming home anyway?" I asked her.

"I'm not sure yet, but I'm a quit playing and get a test today. And coming home?? You bounced out I heard. You coming back?" she didn't let me answer. "I didn't think so bitch, so don't try to encourage me to. Anyway, me and Gerald gone start us a family here. This is my home now."

She keeps going. "He should be back any day now. He been gone for a little over a week, but that's the normal time for him. But, I heard about what happened between Enoch and Jay. That's real fucked up!" she responds. Something was definitely wrong with Kelly. I could hear it in her voice. She didn't sound the same.

"Are you okay? You don't seem to be yourself." I told her.

"Yeah girl I'm straight. Always honey. You and sis should come up here so y'all can see what is really cracking' on the west coast," she replied.

"Girl, a vacation is the farthest thing from my mind right now. I may be dying a slow death!" I was crying again.

We talked for an hour and some. She finally told me that Gerald was a pimp, which I already knew. He was like Don Juan with all the gold and furs. She let it all out telling me they had one big house, but she slept with him because she was the main chick. I thought to myself, *No Kelly that is because you are the newest addition.*

She talked about how all they did was party, get high, drunk, and fuck. That was really the same shit we did at home. I was tired of doing the same shit, but I guess she wasn't.

As Kelly talked the more and more her true feelings came out. She explained to me that she already knew she was pregnant, but didn't know if she wanted to keep the baby or not. She didn't even seem to give a fuck what happened either way. *But why not? What happened to her that she changed like this? Was he beating her? Was she on drugs heavy?* I am pretty sure he had her whoring, too! Nobody even really knew that nigga.

"Kelly, can you please just come home?" I asked. "You don't have to live like that with no pimp and his whores!"

"Hell naw I ain't coming home. Bitch, I already told you that. That is the last place I want to come to! I am just fine where I am. My nigga love me! Damn! Everything ain't gone be like no fairy tale, Karter!! Life is not a box of fucking chocolates!" she said to me.

"I mean let's be real! This is just why I never call and why I sure as hell ain't coming back there!" She yelled. She was pissed. *But why?*

"You left so why can't' I stay away?! Do me a favor, Karter, be a friend, cousin whatever, and listen to this will you, DON'T CALL ME EVER AGAIN YOU PUNK BITCH!!!!!"

The line went dead. Something was wrong. She knew I wasn't preaching. I was just concerned. Hell how the fuck was I preaching when I had my own fucked up drama that I was going through. She was tripping. I called Sis to tell her what happened, but she was already calling me.

"How about I was just about to call you to tell you about your crazy ass sister. The chick is off the chain." I told her. "She has to be on something. She ain't never acted like that before.

"Even if she called herself being in love with this pimp what in the world could he do for her, but take her money!?" I was pissed off.

"Niggas like that don't have bitches around for nothing no matter how much of a main chick you think you are! You gotta earn your keep!" I said. "And when I asked her when she was coming home the tramp must a got an attitude and hung up on me!"

My line was clicking from a private caller. I wasn't about to answer that shit. I already knew it was some bullshit. It was either something related to Enoch or it could have been Enoch.

It made me wonder how he was doing? Was he going to make it? What would they charge him with? Did they confirm his diagnosis to him of HIV? I wanted him to stay his bitch ass in jail or just fucking die. If he got out I would have to find him and take care of him. No choice. He was trying to get at me by any means.

I really wanted to knock him off. I was going to try my best to find away before I had to leave. If I did I was going to take care of his bitch ass. Once and for all. I was going off into another land that fast. Sis snapped me out of it.

"Yeah something's not right with her at all! But, I got to go. One of Jay's doctor is here." She told me. "Okay call me later and tell Jay I said hey." I told her. "I will girl," she replied.

Chapter Eleven

Jay was still in ICU. They were talking about possibly taking him out and sending him to the floor. He had a long road ahead of him. He wasn't paralyzed he just had to learn how to do things again. With therapy the doctors said he may have a slight limp if that.

I was for sure going to stop by there before I got back in the air. He and Sis was the only reason I even came back to Kansas City in the first place.

I didn't go back to chill and hang. It was to be supportive to Sis make sure she was good and bounce. You just never know the outcome when someone gets shot.

The tragedy that I went through, and the one that I was partially responsible for, had me thinking about what I really wanted in life. It had me thinking that all the shit I had done was really pointless, because why was I still not fucking happy. *Would killing Enoch make me happy?* I wasn't sure. I did know that as long as Enoch was around he would do anything to make sure I wasn't happy.

I wanted to be happy. I tried to think back to the time I was happy. I tried to remember a time when I enjoyed life. When was it? Did it even exist? Was Kelly right? Fairytales didn't really happen?

I wanted so desperately to recall a memory of me feeling good. I didn't even feel all the way good or right when I was with Enoch. Where was my knight in shining armor? Where was my husband?

I prayed that Enoch wouldn't continue to screw up my life even when I wasn't with him. I was so ready to get back to Atlanta and get on with my "new" life.

I finally got that phone call I had been waiting for and when she told me that my results were negative that was music to my ears. She told me to play it safe and to come back in six months to take another test. I hung up the phone and cried tears of nothing but joy.

I started jumping on my bed like I was a damn five-year-old. I was happy as hell!!! It was like I was given life again. Thank GOD! I wanted to call and tell Kelly that I was negative, but decided against it.

I didn't want to go through anymore shit with her and I sure as hell wasn't going to kiss her ass. Fuck her. I didn't feel like the drama with her punk ass anyway.

I wanted to run out of my hotel room and scream and yell that I was not positive. I got up, got dressed, and rolled the fuck out. My flight was scheduled to leave the next day, late afternoon. That day, I was determined to make the best of. I had no intentions on returning to that city anytime soon.

I didn't have too many loose ends to tie up so I could do what it was I needed to. Aside from seeing Jay and Sis again there wasn't much. I needed that one day to celebrate or just reflect on the scare I had just had.

Plus, I knew that when I got back to Atlanta it was all work no play. I needed to get it all out of my system. I was feeling really good. I had money in my pocket and I was starting a new life.

I was so very happy I didn't have HIV. I knew I still needed to play it safe like the doctor said and I planned to. I didn't have anybody I was fucking. I didn't have a man. I had thought about going to find me a girlfriend.

Maybe I wasn't having any luck with men because I was really supposed to be with a woman. Hell a lot of memories with Enoch included me getting and being high.

I just can't recall the emotion or feeling at some of those times because of the numbness. I guess that was the only way I was able to get through some things. All the shit was easier to endure when I was out of it.

I made it back to Atlanta in one piece. Time seemed to fly as soon as I touched. I kept myself busy and got right back on my grind. I went to beauty school during the day and business school at night. The beauty school I went to was Anita's and the night school was at the community college.

I was also able to help out at one of her businesses. She had a boutique that recently opened and it worked around all my class hours. With the job and going to school I was busy as hell. I was good with that. I kept myself occupied.

I remember when I was little my great aunt used to always say an idle mind is the devil's workshop. That's some real shit. It was so fucking true. It was like since I had something to do I didn't have the cravings all the time. I wasn't tripping off of the fast life or club scene. I was over it.

I had been to a few spots and they were cool as hell. I thought I had to have all of that in my life, but I was wrong. I liked the flashy shit, but I didn't like what I had to do in the past to get all of it. I didn't have time to even think about small things, let alone think the way I was before moving to Atlanta, and while I was with Enoch.

I had finally gotten my own spot. It was the shit, too. A brand new townhome. It was right outside of Atlanta, but I had everything around me. Not far from either school, and the boutique was even closer.

It had been a minute and I still hadn't talked to Kelly since she hung up on me. I was worried about her and I really missed her. I wanted to know how she was doing. I wanted to tell her that I wasn't dying after all.

Fuck it! Unlocked my phone and dialed her Kelly's number. The subscriber is not accepting calls at this time. *Now was her phone disconnected by the provider or did she just change her number? Now I was really worried!!*

There my girl was thousands of miles away and I had no way of contacting her. What the fuck was going on with her and where in the hell was she? I just prayed that she was okay and that she wasn't really pregnant. That would only complicate things more.

The sad messed up part about it was none of the women even seen half of what they sucked and fucked for. Kelly was one of the younger whores at that, she wasn't fully aware of how all this shit went. The pimp and hoe stuff was some dirty shit.

I mean really you do all these sexual things to somebody you may never see again, get paid for it and then give it all to your so called pimp. All the while still respecting and being loyal to him! Ha! But at the same time, it sounded so much like what I did on a regular basis while I was with Enoch!

I was actually living a normal life in Atlanta. The first for me. It wasn't hard, though. I had plenty of shit to do so I didn't have time for nonsense. I also had money coming in on a regular basis so I didn't have to pull licks and shit. I was good.

I invested some money with Anita on two different projects. One was an apartment complex and the other was the boutique. Since I pretty much ran it, I started to manage it and put my money in it.

Basically I owned that store franchise. It was her name, but my money made it flow so majority of the return was mine. She just got a percentage. It was a win, win for me. I didn't even have to work as much there because I was the BOSS.

One thing however didn't change was the fact that I kept getting them dumb ass private calls. The shit was so fucking annoying. They would just call and hold the phone or breath really hard. Sometimes I didn't answer them at all. I had no idea who it was. I didn't know if it was one of Enoch 's chicks or not. Or just a random stalker.

I didn't know if it was Enoch himself or not. I was still low key spooked about his home boy in Dallas that we knocked off. *What if it was related to that?* It was not my intention to be present while he shot and murdered his friend. Even though I knew nothing about his plan, I was guilty by association. I was a damn witness.

Word on the street was that Enoch had infected a lot of people and they were looking for him. So, that told me two things: One he knew he was positive, and two he was not locked up. I'm sure he was on the run somewhere. *But where?* I wondered but knew he could have been anywhere. I couldn't help but have that feeling he was still on his mission to get me.

He was out on bond for the shit with Jay and they kept continuing it. The other guy he was with never got out. They were already looking for him to charge him a double homicide from a few months ago.

I don't even know how Enoch had that much money to even bond out. I bet he put up bunny's house or maybe the one he so called owned in Wyandotte County Kansas. It could have been a chic that posted his bond. Hell with his track record it could have been a nigga!

It really didn't matter because that bastard would probably never go back to court. He would prolong things and run for as long as he could. He would never turn himself in. I was sure he had some money somewhere and if not he would find a way to get it.

I was still pissed and hurt behind all that shit. I was even more so pissed because I believed that he been knew that he was positive and was trying to infect me with it intentionally.

That shit makes me want to just knock him off even more. Why would you purposely pass some shit on to somebody like that?? Why wouldn't you at least tell the person you fucking you got it?!

With the advancements in the medical field and so much research on AIDS/HIV, they have found shit to prevent you from getting it besides, just condom use. I loved him that much that I would have taken that once a day pill, used the suppository gel, whatever I needed to do to prevent myself from getting infected. It's messed up because he didn't give me the choice, either.

If I felt like this and I hadn't contracted it from him; I could only imagine how the people felt who he did infect. Enoch and I never used a condom. That's why I wasn't surprised when I found out I was pregnant. Well actually I was, but it was because that was the last thing on my mind. I knew he and I never used protection and I was on no type of birth control.

Things happen for a reason. Or so that's what everybody always said. At that point in time I didn't understand the reason. I had no clue why all of those things had happened the way they did.

I sure as hell didn't know how things would play out. Life was a hell of a thing. All the shit you had to endure and experience was wild. Only to get through it or over it and have yet another thing come up.

There was another saying that stuck with me as well, "Keep living." I didn't understand what that meant before. Later, I understood exactly the meaning. Keep living and you will keep going through shit, and that shit I was dealing with was crazy. Every time I would reflect on it, it seemed to get crazier and crazier.

The good thing was one unhealthy individual had been removed from my life. He was gone and I would do anything to keep it that way. He needed to stay as far away from me as he could.

I was just starting to get over the whole being scared and afraid of him thing. I was starting to really comprehend just how dumb I had been for him and that really pissed me off.

At the time I just thought it was because I loved him so much. But, him in the other hand, he didn't give two fucks. His actions spoke so much louder than his words. Enoch used who he could for what he could. With no regard for anyone. That type of shit made me want to fuck his ass up. Like whoop his ass again.

Then, I would think about how much I had done and accomplished to better my life in the short time I had been away from him. I wasn't about to fuck that up, either. He needed to stay far the fuck away from me and my life. I would play no games with him. That was on me. I was in the process of shaking things off. I would end his life with the quickness if I had too.

At that moment in my life I wasn't sure what a healthy relationship was and what it looked like, especially for me. Relationships of any kind were tricky for me. My ex, my mom, and Kelly.

My circle wasn't large so that said a lot about me. The relationship I was nervous about at that point, I hadn't even yet started. That was the one with Judah. I was a nervous fucking wreck and he hadn't called. I wasn't sure if he ever would, either. What I did know is that I hadn't stopped thinking about him since I meet him.

I didn't know if it was because I was just horny as fuck or if I sort of had a crush. He was handsome as hell. His frame was on point. Tall and lean. Caramel complexed.

His beard was shaved perfectly and he seemed attentive. That short amount of time I spent with him was like a dream. That was some shit I don't think I had ever experienced. I knew I for sure wanted him to talk to him again. I wanted to see what he was really about. *Was he different?*

Chapter Twelve

One Saturday morning early before I had even opened my eyes for the morning my phone rang and woke me up out of my sleep. I tried to glance at the display, but my eyes were still a little blurry. So I just slid the screen to answer.

As soon as I heard the voice on the other end of the phone I woke up all the way and sat up straight in the bed. My heart started to beat fast. It was Judah. His voice alone had me on cloud nine with bubble guts. *Damn.*

We talked for a while. I had to ask him to repeat himself many times during the conversation, but it was still a great conversation. We didn't even talk about shit. Just laughed and vibed. It was different, but I liked it.

He told me that he called me plenty of times since he first met me, but I never answered. He said that he was no longer in Kansas City, but planned to come back soon. He wanted to take me out when arrived.

I was somewhat confused initially because I just assumed he lived in Kansas City since the restaurant was the family business. I assumed wrong. He explained that he was in Atlanta at that time and he, in fact, spent quite of bit of it there in the A.

I told him that I was in Atlanta right then as well. I was somewhat hesitant because I thought it was ironic that he was there and so was I. I started getting paranoid and shit. *What if he is a set up? What if he a brother or something of a person I jacked or set up? What if he is the dead homie people?*

I was bugging. *What if he was sent by Enoch?* I had to tell myself to calm the hell down and stop tripping. I snapped out of my daydream zone and engaged back in the conversation. He was shocked as well and thought it was a hell of a coincidence. I wasn't sure if I believed in those or not. Because didn't every fucking thing happen for a reason?

I told him I would love to go out with him. We ended the phone call with a date planned for that evening. I gave him the address and told him I would be ready at 7:30pm. It didn't matter. If he was out to get me I would find out now. Better sooner than later.

I lit the blunt I had from the night before in the ashtray and instantly started to prepare for the date. I was still floating. He was something I wasn't used to. He was different.

I didn't know where the hell we were going. He told me, "Mi wan par wit u." That meant to just spend time with a person. You know hang out and party with someone. I was good with that. I wanted to get out and in traffic, anyway. I for damn sure would enjoy being his arm candy.

The fit I had was the perfect occasion for it. I decided on a cute ass outfit I had been dying to wear from the boutique. This is the perfect opportunity. Out on the town with your man. *Oops! Um wait. Not so fast, Karter.* I was moving way too fast. Just a minute ago I was spooked about telling him I was in the same city he was. Then, the next minute he is my man. I had to get my life.

I continued to get my clothes and everything else I would wear out. As I looked through the cloths in my closet I found a few other items that I hadn't worn. I pulled them out as well.

I had to make sure I was ready and on point. A sexy, but versatile outfit. Couldn't go wrong with a pair of black studded peep toe heels, a bad ass body con, and a black Chanel handbag.

By the time I straightened up the house, made some runs, and checked on the boutique it was time for me to start getting ready. Time had flown by and I was excited. I was a little nervous about the date. I hadn't been on one in a while. I sure as hell had no clue about him.

I had to find somebody who knew him. I made sure to make a mental note to ask Anita and my cousin about him. I needed some insight into who he was. Needed a little background from the streets on him.

I went to the bathroom and started to clean the tub again and run some bath water. As I continued my ritual of getting ready, I wondered where we would go. How was it going to feel being out with a dude that wasn't a mark and not Enoch? Was I sure I was ready to get back out there again?

My mind continued to race as I bathed and got ready. Then, all of a sudden I had this overwhelming urge for some coke. *What the fuck?* Why in the hell did that feeling come at that time? Why did it just come up like that? I had to figure out what my triggers were. I didn't know if I was able to change them or not, but at least I would be prepared when whatever the trigger was happened, came, or I ran across it.

I kept moving. I put everything on. I grabbed my clutch and put a little makeup on. I kept it simple. Mascara, lip gloss and was ready!! Purse in hand, fully dressed with shoes on, I did a once over in the mirror to make sure I was on point. I was clean.

Classy and cute. I headed out of my bedroom, but before I got to the door I stopped in my nightstand and grabbed several of the condoms the doctor's office had given me. I had to be prepared just in case. You never know what the night would bring.

The doorbell rang. I was super surprised when I heard it go off. Not because I didn't know who it was, but because I wasn't use to that. I was used to a nigga calling and saying he outside or shit, a "honk honk". Like I'm here. Come on. I was so not used a guy coming to the door for me. Seems I had to possibly get used to something else beside the way he talked.

When I met him at the front door, he greeted me with a hug. He smelled so fucking good. He asked me if I had everything. I told him yes. He asked me was I ready I told him I just needed to lock the door. I did just that and turned back to him.

He grabbed my hand and lead me to where his car was parked. I had no clue what car he was in, nor did I know where we were headed. I was nervous and excited at the same time. I was curious, but scared. I wasn't used to going out with a man for just pleasure. Every time Enoch and I went out it was to scope out the scene to find out who the next mark was.

We approached his car. It was a blacked out Audi 8. Hmmm!! I said to myself. This is nice and new. I wondered what all he was into. He opened the passenger door for me. He smiled at me. I smile back and got in. *Is he always this way or is this just a front?* I thought.

He walked around and got in the driver's side. He asked me to buckle up and I obliged. He started the car and we proceeded to leave from my townhomes subdivision. He started some small talk by asking me how I was doing. I let him know I was doing well. He told me I smelled good. I told him he did, too.

I sat back and enjoyed the ride. I was just ready to enjoy myself and have some fun. I meant to bring my flats to put on afterwards. I really didn't like walking in heels wobbling or walking barefoot to the car and shit after the club. Not classy at all! It was too late at that point.

I needed to keep my heels on any way that night. My ass was short, but I felt even shorter compared to him. I stood five foot exactly. I had to wear heels when I went out. I kept looking over at him as he was driving.

I normally didn't go for guys with dreads, but it was something about him. He had a nice length and they were well maintained. I don't think it would have even mattered how his hair was. I was attracted to him.

As we were riding, he pulls out a fat ass joint, and fires it up. *My type of guy!!!* He takes a puff after puff, but didn't offer me any. I started to quietly get offended. I didn't know if I should ask or should I just let it go. I wanted to hit his weed, though.

It smelled super good. Maybe they didn't like woman to smoke. Maybe he didn't want me to. Awe shit. I could not be with another controlling ass dude. I wouldn't be able to do that one. No way no how. I stopped thinking about it and just asked him to hit his joint. He opened the ashtray and handed me another joint only a little smaller.

He explained that he didn't like to smoke after people. "Tew manty germs dem," he said. I said, "Oh okay well do you kiss?" He tells me yes but not that much.

He said it's different when you kissing your woman versus putting your mouth on the same joint as another trifling nigga. I started to laugh. That was also a new one for me. Most niggas I knew didn't give a fuck whose mouth had been on it. They wanted to get high.

I lit up the joint that he gave me and took a long drag. I started to cough instantly. That was some heat for real. He let out a little chuckle. When I stopped coughing I told him not to laugh at me.

He didn't pay me no mind. I was high as hell and so was he. We both kept hitting our joints. Riding. Chopping it up. It was some good weed and it had me on my level. It seemed like we were driving forever, but I didn't care. I needed to get out of the house and enjoy myself for a change.

A few things I had learned about him in that short amount of time was that he was different and he was gentleman. So far he had major points. We talked as he drove. I asked him if he was in a relationship. I thought I had better get that part out of the way before I got caught up in some shit.

He told me he was not in a relationship and that the last one ended a little while ago. He said he didn't have any kids. But he did want at least three. I wondered what happened between him and his ex. He seemed like a cool dude. He told me she was American. He said he hasn't dated a Jamaican woman since he was young and lived in Jamaica.

"Mi affi mek one more stop for we reach," he says to me. I told him okay. I wasn't tripping 'cause I enjoyed our conversation and his company. I found out he was thirty-two and worked for his family. He explained that his father started a few businesses when he came to the states years ago.

But, his father has since retired and he runs things. He told me that his mother and father were still alive and still together. He said they have a house in Jamaica as well so they spend time there also.

I was shocked about the whole no kids thing. I didn't know too many dudes that looked that fine and that age who didn't have kids. I thought Enoch didn't have any kids, either, but many came out of the woodwork. I didn't think niggas with no kids even existed anymore. I didn't know why I was so surprised shit I didn't have any kids. It was a close call, though.

Chapter Thirteen

We stopped by the gas station and met this older looking guy. He handed Judah an envelope, they shook hands, and we were back on our journey again. We ended up at the hottest comedy club in the city.

It was called "Big Laughs". They always had the bomb comedians, but I had never been to an actual show before just the club downstairs afterwards when I first got to ATL. I was nervous as hell, but I didn't show it. A grown woman never does.

"Yuh ready?" Judah asks me as he turns the ignition off.

"Yes I am." I say back to him. "I assume we are going to the comedy show so who is the comedian that is performing tonight?"

"Ricky Smiley." He replies.

"Who?" I ask him.

"Yuh soon see." Was all he said back to me.

I looked in the rearview mirror and put on my lip-gloss. I didn't even notice that he had come around to my side. He opened the door for me and helped me out.

We get to the door and it was a long ass line. It was wrapped around the joint. He grabbed my hand and we walked right to the front of that bitch. On our way to the top of the stairs where the line began all eyes were on us.

We reached the top of the steps and the guy that took the tickets said, "We got yo spot ready." Then, he asked me, "How are you this evening, lovely lady?"

"Fine thank you," I said.

"I know how you look I asked how you were?" he quickly said. He was American. He didn't have an accent.

"Aye mon. Stop yuh chat to mi gurl and do yuh job." Judah says with a little smirk and we head toward the door.

We entered the auditorium and a few staff members that were standing by the door tried to hurry and act busy as soon as we walked in. The way they acted you would have thought Judah was the man, the boss, or something.

He still hadn't let go of my hand as we headed to our seats. We approached our spot and it was obvious why they were the best ones in the house. There were tables and chairs everywhere and booths. We were right in the center and still really close to the front.

We sat down and scooted to the middle of the booth. No sooner than we placed our asses on the seat did one of the waitresses come over with this little attitude.

"I'm Joann and I will be your waitress tonight," she said while she looked at me. Then, she looks at Judah.... "What can I get this lovely COUPLE tonight?" she asks.

"I would like water for now." I replied. I was parched as hell.

"Bottle of Monet." He told the waitress.

"I will have those drinks right out." She said to us and walked off.

I noticed the entire time she was taking our order she kept looking at Judah. She must have been digging him or wanted to fuck him, or already had, and was mad about it. Either way she had better back the fuck up, because I was with him that night. I was already starting to enjoy myself.

I was excited about the fact that I had never been to a comedy show and I was there with this fine ass nigga with the best seats in the house! Shit it couldn't get no better than that at the time. As long as I had been with Enoch he had never done anything like that for or with me.

"Why yuh nah talk much?" Judah asked.

"No reason. Just taking everything in. I really like this set up. I am starving, though. Is the food here good?" I asked him.

He tells me, "Ya mon! It's good."

I looked over the menu to see what I wanted to order. Just as I looked up from the menu, Joann arrived. She puts our drinks down on the table and I immediately start drinking my ice cold water. *So refreshing!* As I am downing my water I noticed her staring at my boy again.

That time I asked her was she waiting to take our order. She snaps out of it and asks us what we wanted to order and places her eyes right back on Judah. I let her know that we need a few more minutes so she can come back. She walks away.

Judah looks down at his vibrating phone on the table and says to me. "Gimme one min. Mi affi tek dis call." He takes the phone call. He gives the person the directions to the comedy house.

He also told them complete instructions as to who they should hand whatever it was they had to. He said okay and ended the call. I understood just about everything he said on that phone call. It seemed that at times his accent was thicker than at other times. Since he was off the call I talked to him about the wandering eyed waitress.

"Damn, ya girl got the hots for you! You must come here often?" I say to him.

"Someting lik dat. Mi part owner," He said.

What the fuck?! That explains all of the extra attention, all the stares and whispers and the best damn seat in the house. My mind raced. All that came across my eye lids was $ $ $ when I closed my eyes. We continued small talk ordered our food, ate, and laughed our asses off at the comedian. He was a funny dude.

When the show was over we stayed afterwards. I assumed to party down stairs at the club, but once again I assumed wrong. We were going to a totally separate club. It was us, the comedian, and a slew of other people who I did not know.

As we stood around talking and mingling the same cat that was flirting a little with me on the way in, handed him a white envelope. He put it in his pocket and continued to socialize.

They did it so smooth each time it happened, it was unnoticeable. I pay attention so I for sure peeped it. They did the little hand shake embrace, semi hug stuff and exchanged them that way. I wondered what was in those envelopes.

We went to this club called The Palace and we had VIP action from the moment we pulled up. The club was off the chain. It was huge with like three floors and at least two bars on each level. TV's everywhere, even in the booths.

That was my type of club!! We had bottles popping and of course the best service. I could get used to all I had experienced that night. I had kicked it before no doubt, but the way he kicked it was different. It was fun as hell, but it was still different. It was like, since he had money he partied different.

I didn't care, though. I was surprised, but digging the fact that me and him was vibin like we were. I went to the restroom to relieve myself and check my face in the mirror. Make sure my hair was on point, too. I fixed my shit, put my lip gloss on, and sprayed a few sprays of my perfume! I was ready.

When I got back to the VIP section, Judah was in the circle booth looking hella good. I walked right over to him and sat down. He started to say something to me, but I didn't even give him a chance to finish. I kissed him and before we both knew it we was spooning the hell out of each other. The chemistry was definitely there between me and Judah. There was no doubt.

His hands were wandering all over my body. I was loving every minute of it. We were damn near fucking. That's how intense the "make out" had gotten. His shirt was up and his hand was under mine. I felt him up.

I wanted to know what I would potentially be working with. I wasn't the type of chick who was scared of the dick. I wanted it. But, I wanted it to be right. I didn't have time for a short man. I couldn't do it. I needed to feel it.

"We can't do this here." I said as I stopped for air.

"How cum wi caa?" he responded.

"Cause everybody can see." I said to him.

"Mi whan u." He told me. We managed to get that out between kisses, rubs, and feels. I was having the time of my life with Judah that night. I wanted it to last forever.

We finally stopped our smooching and got ourselves together. *Damn I want this nigga!!!* I was just staring at him and he was staring right back. We were looking in one another's eyes and we were close as hell.

But we had to be in order to hear each other. I still couldn't believe all this was going on inside the damn club. It was like we were in our own world because it was somewhat secluded.

"What is this game? Who will blink first?" I ask him in a rather loud voice. I wanted to make sure he heard me over the music.

"Na. Mi jus tink u a beautiful!" he said.

I was speechless for a moment. He seems a little deep to me. Just his vibe told me that. I really didn't know how to respond to what he said. Young Joc was blasting in the background. "I know you see it!" So, I took my chance to break the trance and deep thought I was in.

"I know you see it!" I said to Judah playfully with a big smile on my face.

"Yeah mi do!!" He said to me looking down at my pussy. "Mi waan see dem pum pum."

I instantly started blushing. It was vulgar, but I liked that shit. What woman didn't want a man to want her? I am sure some would have found that very disrespectful, but it did just the opposite for me.

That shit turned me on. I was extremely attracted to that man. Seemed like since the first day we meet. I wanted him and I wanted him bad.

Then, I thought about the shit I had just been through. I thought about the scare I had just had. Was I really positive and I just didn't know it. *Karter, chill the hell out!* I told myself. I was all worked up for nothing. She also said that before you are intimate with a partner they should be tested to know their status as well.

The time came where the club closed and we bounced. I was still amped. I had really enjoyed myself. I had real fun. I reflect on myself, and I noticed that I wasn't strung the fuck out.

That was the reason I had so much fun. I went out often and I did similar things and had been in VIP before. But this time I was not using. I had a clear head. I was in tune.

It's messed up I had to get my ass beat bad enough to be in the hospital in order for me to stop snorting coke. I normally didn't go out, anyway. That was Enoch's thing. I never went to just enjoy myself. It was always an agenda for me. Never leisure.

We reached Judah's car. He opened the door for me and I got in. He walked around and got in on his side. He immediately reached in the middle console and grabbed another already rolled joint.

Judah seemed to have it fucking going on. But what the fuck did he do? Was he even legit? I didn't need to be fucking with no nigga that was in the game, especially that heavy that he was pushing a whip like his, owning clubs, bars, and shit. But, why would I want one that wasn't balling out of control? If you gonna do it, you may as well do it big right?

I was so deep in thought that I didn't even realize that we had been driving that fast. It seemed we got to the Waffle House quick! We got out, went in, and took our seats. The waiter comes over and we ordered. We got our food, ate, and talked.

He explained more about the last relationship he was in. From what he said she was out of the picture. Although, she didn't want to be. That's what they all say. But, if that was truly the case then that bitch just lost her spot completely.

It was being filled immediately and permanently. *Damn let me slow my ass down. I just met this nigga and I'm trying to be his woman already. I barely even knew him. What was I thinking?* We hadn't even got down yet, which was probably a good thing, but how long would it last?

He seemed cool but was it just be a front? He told me that he traveled a lot because he had his hands in just about everything.

He did most of his traveling in the states, but overseas every now and then. So, literally I was fucking with a nigga that's worldwide. That shit turned me on even more.

By the time we were done jaw jacking and stuffing our faces the sun was coming up. We left with Judah in the driver's seat again. My phone rang. Private number again. I didn't even contemplate answering it. I simple silenced it and kept right on chilling and riding.

We had the music blasting, Judah holding the lit joint. He passed it to me. I hit it two puffs and passed it back. It was about gone so another one needed to be rolled. He told me to opened the glove compartment. I did.

There was about an ounce of weed, some papers, and the prettiest damn gun I had ever seen. I grabbed the weed, the papers, closed it, and started to breakdown the weed to roll the joint.

"Judah, where we are going now? Where are taking me?" I asked. He responded with, "Don't worre ya self. Mi got u."

I rolled two more joints at that point just to make sure we kept the train going. That was exactly how he smoked, like a damn freight train, and I wasn't too far behind him. The papers he smoked were not harsh, either.

We stopped, got gas and bottled water, then we were off again. I guess he wanted to stay hydrated. I had no earthly idea what our destination was. But, I was excellent at following directions so I just sat back, got blazed, and enjoyed the ride.

Chapter Fourteen

We ended up at his loft downtown. It was extravagant, over the top! I mean this bitch was plushed out. Had a door man and all. *Did I hit the jackpot or what?!* I was exhausted and revved up all at once. I needed a nice hot bath with candles lit to calm me down and relax me. I was excited. I didn't know what to expect at that point. I was a big girl though, so I could handle whatever.

"I like your spot. It's dope. How long you been living here?" I asked him, trying not let the excitement be heard in my voice.

"Mi just here a short time," he said. As I was looking around the rest of his place. He asked me if I needed anything. I told him no and he said he would be back soon. He went up the stairs and I just chilled on his couch.

I made myself comfortable. I took my shoes off and relaxed. Just as I was letting out a deep breath I felt his presence in the room. He only had a wife beater and boxers on. He was cut. His physique was on point!!!!

He walked over to me and grabbed my hand. He guided me up off the couch and up the spiral staircase. He didn't say a word and neither did I. I just followed his lead. As we made our way, I could hear the music he had playing. It was low. It was **Maxwell's A Woman's Work**. That song was one of my favorites
.

As we arrived to his bedroom he turned and looked at me. I didn't know what the hell he was about to do next, but I sure wanted to know so I just stood there with him. In silence as the music played. I looked up at him and our eyes locked. He leaned in and started to kiss my lips softly. He grabbed my waist and moved my body in closer to his. *Damn this man felt good!* I thought to myself.

My hands began to wander all over his body. His skin was smooth and soft. His muscles were thick and firm. I touched his manhood and it was like a fucking rod. His hands did the same on my body. I enjoyed every minute of it.

The way he slid his hands down the small of my back passed my ass and stopped right where he could cuff it. He lifted me just a little that I had to stand on my tippy toes and he brought me closer at the same time. *I was going to fuck the shit outta him.*

Just as I was starting to get aroused he stopped and just looked at me, studying my face. I was really worked up. I had to calm down. I broke the silence.

"Do you mind if I bathe?" I asked him. "Yuh ca do whatever yuh like. Mi nuh mind at all." "Yuh nee mi ta wash ya body dem?" He asked.

I told him whatever he wanted to do. *I would love that.* I thought. He took my hand and led me to the bathroom. It was huge in there.

It was decorated very well and everything had its place. The bathroom was a sleek modern look. Everything was grey, white, and silver. The towels that hung on the racks for decoration were white.

The tile in shower and on the floor were grey and it was dope. All of the fixtures were silver and didn't have a fingerprint on them. It was very clean too.

I really liked the artwork on the walls. It was impressive. I looked at the type of toilet stool he had as well as the quality of towel he had hanging on the racks. He had that cake.

It was some expensive shit in that house. He probably had a safe. *Karter, chill the hell out!!!* I had to remember that I was not out to get this dude. I had to remember that this could be my man.

He was on that level. Plus, I didn't want or need a damn thing from him. I was doing well for myself. I would not be in a trick bag again, that was damn for sure.

He sat me down on this small seat that was next to the tub. I sat and watched him as he ran the water, put the bubbles in, and lit the candles. As the water ran he undressed me. He took his time and every part of my body he touched was gentle, soft yet so enticing.

Once I was completely naked he took my hand and helped me in the bath tub. The water was hot as hell, but that was just the way I liked it. I laid my head back and closed my eyes. He must have known I needed to be left alone because he just walked out of the bathroom without saying another word.

It was nothing for me to take my clothes off in front of a man. I basically did that for a living. I mean maybe not every day 9-5 type shit, but I showed my body to men I had just meet just to rob their ass. He was different, though. It was something about him. I was surprised he walked out of the bathroom.

He was being a gentleman and that I was not used to. As a matter of fact, he had been a gentleman all night. Opening my door, making sure I sat down first, and allowing me to order first. The whole nine. He even rang the doorbell when he picked me up.

Just as that thought crossed my mind, I felt Judah walk back into the bathroom. As the night progressed he had on less and less. His cloths came off quick. Before I knew it he was booty butt naked, sliding in the tub behind me.

He was a nice sized nigga. His body was on point. He was stacked. He wasn't like a body builder thick, but he was cut. He looked like he weighed around 210 pounds give or take a few. Once he was settled in behind me close, I rested my head back on his chest. *I am luvin every minute of this!!!!* I thought.

I closed my eyes once again and instantly I started to reflect on the night. How much fun and enjoyment I had had, on top of the fact that since I had moved from KC I didn't have any fucking drama.

That was something that I got used to fast and was happy about. Then, there I was being spooned from behind by Judah in his Jacuzzi tub. I liked him. He seemed to have his shit together and our conversations were of substance.

As we sat in the tub we smoked and talked for a while. But, when I noticed the water temperature start to change I reached for the washcloth so I could wash up and get out. He stopped me.

"Mi do dis." He whispered in my ear. All I managed to get out was, "Okay." He motioned for me to stand up. I did and so did he. He took the washcloth lathered it up and washed my entire body. He even washed behind my ears and in between my toes. I was on cloud nine. After he was done I did him the same way.

As my hands went over his chest, arms, and back, I was aroused. I thought of the many ways I would let him hit it. By the time I reached his dick my pussy was pouring wet. I wasn't sure how long I would be able to hold myself back.

That nigga was the shit. He was packing. As I rubbed the washcloth over his dick with my right hand, I stroked it with the left, it grew harder and harder with every stroke.

I sure did not want the dick to go to waste. I couldn't. I wanted him bad. It was hard, thick, and long. My pussy was wet and throbbing. Rubbing the dick of a fine nigga like that had me turned the fuck on. I wasn't sure if I was going to be able to prevent myself from jumping on the dick right there in the tub.

We used the detachable shower head and rinsed each other off. He got out first. He grabbed a towel and handed it to me. He then took the next one and tied it around his waist.

Once it was secured he took the towel I was holding and dried me off. I was loving all of the attention. He made me feel like I was special. That was a wonderful feeling. It made me all warm and fuzzy inside. Every touch made me want him even more. That was some shit.

He reached in one of the drawers attached to the bathroom vanity, got out a tooth brush from a pack, and handed it to me. Judah let the water out of the tub, and then used the other sink. He brushed his teeth as well. I was done first.

I gathered up my dirty clothes and walked into the bedroom. There was classical music playing. I didn't have anything to change into so I just sat on the edge of the bed while I waited for him to come into the room. I was amped, but was trying to hold it together. I was ready to attack him. He didn't even realize it. Or did he?

Judah walks into the room with his towel still wrapped around his waist. He asked me if I wanted a massage. I just nodded my head yes without saying a word. He was pampering me. I liked what he did and how he treated me. *But was this just an act? Would it change as time went on? Did he even want this to continue? Was it too early for these types of questions?* I asked myself.

He went to the side of the bed. I just knew he was about to pull out a condom and just take the pussy. He didn't, he pulled out the massage oil. That was a first. *Was this nigga trying to turn me out or what?* I thought. He came to the side of the bed I was on and unwrapped the towel from me. He instructed me to lay on my stomach. I did as I was instructed.

He started from my neck and worked his way down my back. All the way down to my toes. He rubbed, massaged, and caressed all of me. After he finished with the back of my body, he told me to turn over. *Oh, my goodness! This cat is off the chain!* He blew my mind. He hadn't even touched the pussy yet and it was as wet as hell.

He was on top of me kissing me softly. He started with my lips, then my neck then my breast. After he placed a few kisses on my lips, I placed my hands on his back and started to caress him. He pulled my arms away from him. He placed both above my head.

He whispered in my ear, "No, my turn now." He kissed my lips again and continued down the rest of my body. He kissed my breast. He kissed my stomach. He reached my belly button and continued on. It was hard as hell not to touch him. Then, he stopped. *Damn why did he stop?*

He stood up and motioned for me to scoot down to the edge of the bed. Once I was where he wanted me, he spread my legs as wide as they would go, and then he just stared at the pussy. Like it was the Mona Lisa or something. Or like he was about to really fuck it up. He kissed my pussy lips and clitoris very softly. I let out a moan. I tried to reach for him.

Once again he moved my hands. He looked up at me and said, "Don't touch dem, just look." He went to work and that nigga put it down. I had never been given oral sex like that before. And I was even more shocked cause I had always heard Jamaican men don't perform oral sex. Maybe he had been in America too long.

To me that was just more of a confirmation that he was trying to turn me out. I came so many times. Over and over again. Back to back. By the time he finished with me I literally was lethargic. I was done. He laid in the bed beside me and I was out! I slept so good. I woke up happy as fuck!!

I was being held tight in Judahs arms from behind. He must have been waking up too. I felt his dick getting rock hard and I was ready for it. All of it. I wanted all of it inside of my pussy.

The way he pleasured me and put me to sleep I was ready for him to pound the pussy. Beat it up. I turned over, straddled him, and he reached under the pillow. He had a condom in his hand and started to unwrap it.

Once he had it on I took a hold of his dick and slid it right in. I went up and down on the dick. Moved my hips round and round while I raised my ass up and down. I rode that dick like it was a fucking bull. It was my turn to put in the work.

His dick was so good and I had an orgasm out of this world. We came together. He sat up and held me while we both busted. It was the best I ever had. It was a done deal. I was turned out. *I'm s-p-r-u-n-g!!!* I thought. Where the fuck had he been all my life? *Shit!*

Chapter Fifteen

Judah was the shit!! He didn't miss a beat when it came to me and our relationship. Enoch and his bullshit was the farthest thing from my mine. Judah and I were together all the time. If he was in town and wasn't busy and I wasn't at school or work we were together.

He cooked for me sometimes and didn't mind doing it. He made sure I was okay all the time. He would just pop up out the blue and take me to lunch or call me to tell me he was thinking of me. I loved that shit. Hell I loved him. It was like he was happy to make me happy.

I didn't know how to embrace it at first. I was still nervous and wondered what his motive was. I also didn't have time for anybody to be using me or playing games with me.

I had enough of that in my life. I was so used to being used and abused by niggas I almost didn't know that I had a real MAN around me. See I wasn't used to having a man care for me and cater to me. I learned quick to accept it, though. I knew what a good thing looked like when I saw it.

What I wasn't about to have is a man who put the streets and everybody else before me. Shit I didn't even want a nigga in the streets. I was tired of that life and all the shit that came with it. He knew that. He knew because we had had plenty of those deep conversations about life, our dreams and goals.

What we shared was intimate. We opened up to each other. I was honest with him about things. He made me feel secure. At the end of the day I knew what I was getting into when I came to Judah.

I really let my guard down when everything checked out with him. I got the scoop on him from Anita. She said she had to put her ear to the streets but she got the tea. They said he was good. Real type of dude. They said he had that cake. They also confirmed his story of the ex-girlfriend fucking up with him. I of course did not make her a factor.

I learned not to dwell in the past.   The word on the street was she cheated with one of guys that worked for him. He caught them in the act of cheating. They were out on a date together at the same restaurant Juda was picking up a to go order from.

He was about to kill them both but it would have been too many witnesses. His right hand stopped him. He had the gun out and placed right on dudes temple ready to shoot. They were both spared. They were watched over that day.

First thing I thought was, *The nigga is crazy!* But then I realized, when you love somebody it's a whole lot of shit you find yourself doing. Crazy and all.

It was amazing all the stuff you got from the streets. Apparently, the worker left the city. Maybe even the country because he was never heard from again. They said Judah and his family on top of the people he associated with were not the ones to play with.   It seemed that no matter how hard I tried to escape the life, it continued to find me.

Judah's ex-girlfriend was supposedly a model type of chick. They said he loved her and would have married her. He wanted to start a family with her. They hadn't been together in a while, but she still wanted him back. I could never understand why people thought that the grass was greener on the other side.

I didn't need anything from Judah financially and he knew that, but he wasn't intimidated by it at all. He still did for me. He still paid for shit, bought me shit, and gave me money just because. But, what he did not do is try to control me with it.

This was something I wasn't used to either. That was the main way Enoch controlled me. Money and whooping my ass. Since I knew what it felt like to have a man, the BOYS wouldn't be able to fool me again.

I was always daydreaming and couldn't stop thinking about Judah that day the entire time I was at school. Saturdays were normally busy, but for some reason that day went by super slow. I daydreamed about him while I waited for a client to get done drying.

I was so consumed with those thoughts that I didn't even notice the fire trucks across the street near my car. My classmate said, "Karter! Bitch, ain't that your car." I was like, "What???" I snapped out of it and ran outside toward the fire trucks and firefighters. One of them came up to me.

He asked me was that my car. I told him yes as the other fighters worked to put out the flame the car was engulfed in. "Was there anybody else in it or any animals?" he asked. I told him no and explained my car had been parked there since I got to school that morning.

I asked him how it happened. He replied he wasn't sure and wouldn't know anything further until the fire was out and they could do more investigation. I was in utter shock as I looked at my 2009 Camaro going up in flames and being drenched in water by the hoses.

It was black on black with a red stripe down the middle. I liked that car. I really did. I felt the urge to go get high coming on. I fought it off with the reassuring thought of good ole Farmers insurance and the fact that the car was paid for.

I was glad that I had paid my insurance up for a year. After getting so many tickets for no insurance, more trouble and money I didn't have at that time. Let's just say those experiences taught me a good lesson.

I stayed out with the firefighters and police so they could get all my information and let me know the next steps. The officer that took my statement told me that I had to call him back in a few days to get the police report and number. They told me I should have been able to call my insurance company immediately without it.

As I headed back into the school I started to wonder who in the fuck would do that dumb bitch shit to my car? Who knew I was at school? Fuck who even knew me in Atlanta? I knew it had to be a bitch because niggas don't do that. They just come straight for you. Real niggas, anyway. I began to run a list of names that I thought would do some shit like that and why they would.

The list never stopped. All of the people that I had done some shit to had a reason to fucking burn my car up. Bitches that was probably still bitter at me about Enoch. A nigga who didn't like him or didn't like me.

Would they come all the way to Atlanta just to give me a message? What the fuck if that was a warning sign coming from Enoch's friend's people?

I wondered if it was to say to me yeah bitch we know and we know where you at. I was paranoid. That shit was fucked up. Was it a freak accident or a fucking message? I found myself hyperventilating and I knew I had to relax. I took deep breaths. In and out.

I started to get this odd feeling come over me. *This was Enoch!* He followed me down there from KC. He found my ass. I had been so caught up and in love with Judah I forgot all about Enoch's bitch ass. Not anymore. He was right on the top of my thoughts at that point.

The beast in me was wide the fuck awake now. That was a message for my ass. He was taunting me. Enoch was a sore loser. He hated to feel defeated, or conquered. He felt as though he had to always win. Especially when it came to a woman.

Now how in the hell was I going to tell Judah that shit? How in the hell was I going to explain any of it? He would think I was on some scandalous ass, set up artist ass bitch. I was shaking my mutha fuckin head.

Why the fuck wasn't that dude in jail? Why wasn't he fucking dead already from the damn disease? Was he fucking invincible or something?? What the hell?

I left Enoch because I wanted him out of my life and I would have been damned if I let him mess up the one I have newly created for myself. I was going to find his ass and kill him. I had to get him before he got me. But what was I going to tell Judah? At the same time, did I need to tell him anything at all?

One of my classmates offered to give me a ride home after school. I took her up on her offer. Juda was out of town and I didn't even want to worry him. He had to leave on an emergency back to KC.

One of his boys/workers was headed to the bank to make a deposit. On his way he was gunned down and robbed. I didn't ask how much. I wanted him to know I was here for him. I didn't want to add more stress or drill him with questions.

I was nervous as fuck and I wasn't even sure if I wanted him to know. But, how would I explain that my car was gone? It was nothing to lie about. I didn't know who the fuck had did it and that was the honest truth.

I already called the insurance company and filed the claim. It was just hurry up and wait. When I got home all I wanted to do was sleep and try to forget about the fact I wouldn't have a car for a while. I couldn't help but to think, yet again, of all the shit I had done and who I had done it to.

I woke up late that night and calling Judah was the first thing I did. I had to check on him and what went on and make sure I let him know what had happened to me. He was happy to hear from me. I could tell in his voice.

I told him about the car. He said not to worry about it. He said the person may have mistaken it for someone else's. He said it was a few of those in the city and it's possible. I tried to consider that for a split second, and then I was like what about tag numbers.

None of those are the same. He continued to reassure me. He told me that I could get one of his cars to drive so that I could get around, at least until he got back in town.

I didn't say anything about Enoch and the fact that I thought it was him that burned my car up and was more than likely not going to stop until he found me. I didn't tell him that he is after me because I stole money and drugs from him. I didn't tell him that I was going to find him and kill him myself.

I told him I was okay and would get a rental. That was what I paid insurance for. He said okay, but didn't like the idea. He said why get a car from them when he has one I can drive. What was his was mine. But, he respected what I wanted. That characteristic about him was the shit.

Even if he didn't agree with what I did or wanted he respected it. He didn't try to change my mind or force me to do things his way. He was confident in himself. He didn't take me having a mind of my own as disrespect or anything like that.

He never felt like less of a man. He loved that I had a mind of my own. He said a man needs a woman who knows how to make certain decision without her man. Nothing like Enoch's bitch ass. He would have just beaten me, withheld the dope, or money until I did what he wanted.

Judah was reluctant to give me details on his worker. He said that he didn't wanna worry me and that they were handling it. He said that he would be home as soon as they got it under wraps.

He let me know that he was okay, the money was nothing compared to his friend/worker and that the police said they have a suspect. I left it at that. We said our goodbyes and I told him I loved him. He said the same and we ended the phone call. I felt better when I got off the phone with him.

Just as I hung up with him my cell rang with a private number. I never really stopped getting them and I was more inclined to answer it because of the businesses and the car etc. I had a lot going to not answer. It was even later at that time so it had to be important for anybody to be calling. I grabbed my phone and slid it to answer.

"What is it?" I answered sternly.

"It's me.......it's Kelly." She spoke slowly as if she was scared.

"Kelly!?" I replied. I had to make sure I heard her right. I was shocked as hell about the fact that she was on my line. I haven't talked to her since she hung up on me when I was still in Kansas City.

"Yeah it's me. I'm in Atlanta. I-I need a ride from the bus station. Can you come and get me?" she asked me. "I don't have anybody else to call."

"Sure, I can, girl. I'm on my way." I told her.

"Okay..." she paused for a minute. "Thank you, Karter."

Chapter Sixteen

I didn't even have a ride of my own and no one to call myself for one. I couldn't leave her there though. I figured it out fast. I got on my phone and requested an Uber. Once it was confirmed I had a driver, I got dressed and was ready.

The Uber got there in no time. I got in and we headed to the bus station. The bus station was quite a distance from me, so the ride gave me plenty of time to play over in my head how this reunion would go. It allowed me to reminisce on all the good times she and I shared.

Kelly was my best friend, she was my family and I missed her like crazy. I didn't fuck with females, especially in KC. I made a few new friends since I was in ATL. But, nothing like Kelly.

What type of mind frame was she in? I had to remember that she was pregnant by and prostituting for a pimp, possibly on drugs with nothing and nowhere to go. And from the last conversation we had, she was pissed at me. I had no clue where her head was.

The Uber driver finally arrived at the bus station. I asked the driver to wait on me. I told him I was just going to pick someone up. He said no problem. I looked for her in a few different places inside and found her in the bathroom. She came out of the stall. I had to take a double look because I almost didn't recognize her.

Her hair was cut really short just like a boy with a curly bob. Aside from her little pudgy stomach she didn't even look pregnant. She was skinny as hell. She had lost a lot of weight. She looked more like she was three or four months than almost eight. She had to be using something as I suspected. She was just too small.

I walked straight over to her. When I reached her I wrapped my arms around her and squeezed as tight as I could. I was glad my friend and cousin was away from pimping ass Gerald and his whore house.

I missed her. I wanted to cry, but I didn't want her to see me. I had to be strong for her and I needed to see where her head was. Drugs make you do some crazy shit and this could have all been a front.

We made our way back to the Uber, got in, and headed back to my place. I didn't even ask her how she knew I was in Atlanta at that time. I guess she just took her chances since I did live there.

We talked briefly during the ride. I asked her if anyone knew she was in Atlanta? She told me no and she wanted to keep it that way. She didn't seem happy. I wondered why. *Why wouldn't she be happy to be with her loved one? Why wouldn't she be happy to be away from a pimp and what he had her doing? Did she actually miss that shit?*

Then, again she was probably just coming down off of whatever high she was on and was pissed at the world. I could just tell she was using some type of drug. It was all in her face. Besides, why else would she have been so damn small at that stage in her pregnancy?

Whatever the case was, I had to find out where her head was. What did she plan to do now that she was Atlanta? I didn't mind helping anybody as long as they wanted to help themselves. After all somebody was always helping me.

I didn't want to just start drilling her with questions so I tried to allow her to open up and let me know without me asking. I knew she was addicted to drugs and if the fact that she was pregnant didn't make her quit or get help then what would? Hell the real question is does she even want to stop?

She was really, really fucked up, but it was never too late to get herself back together and that is exactly where it had to start. Kelly had nowhere to go.

She was in a city where she knew no one so she stayed with me. I had plenty of room. It was okay for a while. I really didn't mind it. I continued my normal routine and so did Judah.

She did nothing constructive all day. She laid on the couch or in the spare bedroom all day and watched television. She ate everything in sight. As far as I knew she hadn't been using any drugs since she had been in Atlanta. So, that was a good thing. Or had she just been hiding it from me that damn good?

Apparently, she kept it from me and did a great fuckin job at it. That was until she refused to even see the doctor after being there for over a month.

I had learned then she had never even been to any physician her entire pregnancy. She didn't even know how far along she was. If it was a viable pregnancy, nothing.

She claimed she didn't believe or agree with the practices of modern medicine. *What in the fuck was she thinking? How can you not go get care for not only yourself, but for your unborn child?* That was some bullshit to me. She was way far gone.

She thought they were going make her detox. But, they wouldn't have been able to make her only suggest. She sure would have been on the radar to snatch that baby once it was here and with drugs in its system.

I didn't think she cared either way if they had taken the baby from her. A drug addicted baby. Another statistic. I gave her all the information that I had gathered on all the clinics and free services in the city. I let her know that if she wanted to go to let me know, but she never did.

I finally fucking finished school. Hair school itself wasn't hard. I enjoyed it. I loved doing hair and making people look pretty. It was all the other things that I had going on that had my concentration.

Judah, Kelly, and the boutique. I stopped working that other gig. It was too much. Plus, I did well for myself. There was no need for me to have a third job.

Although, I wasn't getting paid while in school my tips was damn good. My customers loved me. I knew what I was doing. I took care of my client's hair and I also laid they shit out.

Natural, relaxed, locs and weave. I did it all and damn well. I had enough clientele to open my own shop and that was exactly what I planned to do next. Karter's lash and beauty salon.

I took the state board test and passed with no problems. That was the best feeling in the world. As a gift from Judah for getting my license he bought me a new car.

I was shocked as hell, but I was like so happy about it. I hadn't replaced mine yet because I couldn't decide what I wanted. He let me drive whichever car of his I wanted for a while, but it's nothing like having your own wheels.

Anyway my baby had hooked me up. He bought me a convertible Benz coupe. Grey with black interior, with the fresh as rims, and banging sound system. That bitch was bad. Damn I loved that man!! And I really liked the car. I was so excited about it.

We got home late after drinking and celebrating. After we made mad love for what seemed like hours we crashed. The next morning I woke up before Judah, so I ordered up breakfast and went to go pick it up. When I didn't see Kelly, I assumed she was in her room asleep. I ordered her something anyway.

I stopped at the gas station and filled my tank up before I picked up our food. I got it, and then headed back home. When I reached the house I went straight to the kitchen and put the food on the counter.

I went to my room to wake Judah up. As I walked to my room I noticed that the door to Kelly's room wasn't shut anymore. I just assumed she was in the bathroom.

Little did I know and would soon find out that the bitch was in my bedroom, seducing my man. I caught the bitch right in the act as I walked in my door.

This hoe was standing at the end of my bed with her robe open saying to him. "I know you want this! Come and get it!" He was still in the bed under the covers barely awake.

I quickly intervened, "No you fucking tramp he doesn't!!! GET the FUCK out of my house, BITCH!!!" I can't believe yo ho ass!!! You really got me fucked up," I said. I was pissed as hell!!! *What the fuck was her damn problem?*

"I was just..." she tried to explain. I cut her right off. "Ain't no explaining the fact you were standing here naked in front of my man. Bitch, in a min we gon' be going toe to toe if you don't get the fuck out. You know how I get down." I didn't even wanna fight her while she was pregnant.

"And, bitch, so do you." That little slut had the nerve to get cocky. "What!?" she said to me like she ready to bang.

That was enough. She didn't have to say or do any more. I was trying not to even put my hands on her because she was pregnant but she had me REAL fucked up. I just stuck the bitch right in her mouth. I beat the fuck out of her.

By this time Judah was up, attempting to break up the fight or should I say ass whooping. He jumped out of the bed naked. He had to scurry around to find pants or something to put on quickly. I kept whooping her ass.

I heard him say, "Bombaclad." That snapped me back into reality. We were fighting like two bitches off of the street who didn't know each other.

I didn't even care about the fact the bitch was pregnant any longer. I tried to kill her. When I caught my breath I said to her. "You had better get the fuck outta my house before I shoot yo ass up outta here!"

"Yeah, whatever bitch." Then, she looked at me like I had shit on my face and walked out. But, how could she be the one mad when she was the one who tried to fuck my man? She really needs to stay off of the shit she was using. It had her mind all fucked up. She was a totally different person.

After that day I told myself I would never let another chick that close to my man again. I don't know what happened to Kelly after that. I didn't hear from her again.

Sis barely heard from her and wasn't even for sure if she made her way back to Kansas City or not. I knew Sis would definitely get a call when she had that baby.

Kelly sure as hell wasn't in the right state of mind to care for a child. She couldn't care for herself, but for some reason Sis seemed to think that she would just let the state have the baby. It didn't seem like she wanted it anyway.

I thought she had too much pride to just give her baby to the state or let them take the baby. She couldn't let everybody know that she was too strung out on drugs to take care of her baby. But when people were strung out who the fuck knew what they would do.

She made that very clear by the shit she tried to pull with Juda. She had no regard for shit. Very small moral compass and little self-respect left. I had been at the point once. I was glad I was no longer there and I hoped like hell she would escape it as well.

Chapter Seventeen

I have never understood why it took so much for a bitch to comprehend when a nigga doesn't want them. What the fuck had to be done for them to get the picture? Does it take something drastic to happen?

Does it take for you to get your ass beat or badly hurt? When I say this ex-girlfriend of Judah's was taking this stalking and harassing thing to a whole new level. The bitch was on Jupiter some damn where.

Estelle was her name and she was still trying to get back with Judah and get rid of me. She wanted her man back. That's how she seen him as her man. I never stopped getting private calls, but I also never figured out who they were from, either.

After hearing that shit I wondered if was she the bitch doing all that shit to me? Was she the one who fucked my car up? Or was it really Enoch? Is she who has been playing on our phones? What the hell is up with this fucking lady? What did Judah do to her?!

I didn't scare easy, but I was tired of dealing with bitches. Fighting, arguing, being petty, and throwing shade. These niggas wanna fuck with you and the next 20 bitches. It was not even worth it sometimes. Enoch sure wasn't worth it.

Judah was without a doubt worth it. On top of it he didn't give me any reason not to trust him. He always made me feel secure in our relationship. That was an unexplainable feeling.

And him I would fight for. I'm not talking about meet up with the girl in the parking lot and start fighting. At the same time I'm not a punk and I would get down, but I had grown so much.

Fighting and arguing was not always the way to handle life. I was talking about standing my ground for my relationship. I wasn't going to just back the fuck up because she felt some type of way. Fuck that and fuck her.

She had better move the fuck around and away from us. I was there to stay. Estelle was not about to run me away all because she fucked up and wanted a do over. That's not always how it worked. She may get a second chance, but she wasn't about to get it with Judah.

I was hired at a top-notch salon once I got my license. The owner liked my work, knew I went to Anita's hair school, and they were cool. She hired me on as a permanent full time stylist.

I loved working there. It was cool as hell. I still planned to get my own salon, just needed not to rush things. Working there let me get some insight on how things operated, what I would do different, and build more clientele.

On this particular day I was completely booked. That was normal for me. Most were regulars and some only came every so often. There were two new faces that day.

This one chick stood out to me for some odd reason. It wasn't her hair because it was beautiful, she wasn't an ugly chick, either. I just had this weird vibe about her.

When I put my finger on it, it was the fact that she talked about her ex-boyfriend the entire time she was there, and from what I gathered he clearly didn't want her. *What the fuck? These chicks are fucking crazy. Always wanting somebody that don't want them.* That shit was unreal to me.

I decided to take a quick break. I went outside in the back to get some fresh air. The crazy new client was already out there smoking a square. I sat down in one of the chairs and just enjoyed the little free time I had out doors in the fresh air. Then, my phone rang. It was Judah.

"Hey, baby!" I answered.

"Waah gwan? Ya busy?" he asked.

"No, never too busy for daddy. What's up?" I replied.

"Mi pon di way ta get a quickie," he said.

"Okay daddy. Please hurry cause I could use one of them." I said. I liked that spontaneous shit.

"Yuh freaky gurl!! But mi don mine sum of yuh poom poom! Mi know yuh busy at work." He was so considerate and he actually remembered most of what I told him.

"I want you to have it." I told him. "You gone be ready for me?"

"Yas sah!" he said. "Alright. Mi wan know wat yuh want for yuh birthday?" he asked.

"I haven't even thought about it baby. How about you just surprise me." I told him.

"Mi surprise yuh naked with a bow on mi cocky," He said, laughing. He always had jokes.

"Real funny Judah! But, I love yo ass and I would sho love that good dick anyway you want to give it to me," I said.

"Mi luv yuh too, gurl! Mi call ya lata. Be ready fa dem rounds," he said.

"I'll be ready." I told him and we hung up.

The whole time I was on that phone call, the new client Tina, was staring straight in my mouth. She was listening to everything I said. This bitch was a freaking weirdo.

Why was she listening to my conversation like that? Why was she all in mine so heavy? Once I got back in, I hurried up, and got her ass out of there. I thought no more about it after she was gone.

I woke up on the day of my birthday and Judah was already gone. He had little notes in different places directing me where to go and what to do. With every note there was pieces of chocolate. He had breakfast made for me and everything. All I had to do was warm it up.

He had a small Prada clutch with one of the notes. It was real cute. Small, but exactly what I wanted. It was perfect. When I got to the end of the little scavenger hunt type expedition, it was a jewelry box.

Inside was an immaculate pair of diamond earrings. My eyes lit the hell up. I was geeked. They looked to be at least 3 carats. I knew by looking at them. I couldn't stop smiling. I immediately put them in my ears. Judah sure knew how to make me happy.

I had to go into work that day so I had to hurry and get ready. I only had three customers because of the fact it was my birthday. I didn't want to be up in there all day. I had to do them, though, they came faithfully to me every week.

Two wash and sets, and then one cut and color. The cut and color was on one of my Latino customers, she would be really quick. Color her, cut her up then blow dry her and she was out.

I was finishing up with my last client just a little after 1 p.m. and I got a text from Judah instructing me to meet him at his place when I left work. *Why didn't he just call me? What did he have up his sleeve?*

I thought. When I was done I rushed to Judah's house. I was amped because I just loved his surprises and I knew he had something fire planned.

When I got to the door I didn't have to knock or use my key. He must have seen me on the surveillance system. When I entered the loft he had candles lit everywhere. They were the scented kind so the house smelled wonderful. He had **Fortunate** by Maxwell playing softly in the background.

There were several bouquets of roses. They were red and white my two favorite colors. On one end of the table he had a chocolate machine with a bowl of strawberries and more exotic fruit next to it. The kicker was a massage table right smack in the middle of it all.

He was in the hallway, looking at me; just watching me grin as was he. It was so beautiful I had tears in my eyes. I had never had this kind of treatment before. *I love this nigga*, was all I could think during the little rendezvous.

The first thing I was instructed to do was allow him to take all my clothes off. He did it slowly and oh so gently. I was stripped down to nothing but my good, new pair of earrings. He handed me a glass of champagne and made a toast to us on my birthday.

After the toast and I was fully undressed, I was told to lie on the massage table. He massaged my entire body started with the scalp of my head all the way down to the tip of my toes.

I was in heaven. It felt so good. It had my body so relaxed I was damn near sleep. I didn't even want to get up. This shit reminded me of the first time we got down.

Damn! Damn! Damn! This man! This man! I am never leaving him!! I loved this man for real! He knew exactly how to treat me and take care of me. He knew just how to get all of my attention and keep it.

Since the first day we met he hasn't slacked up or changed. The person that I fell madly in love with was the same person I was there with that day.

Most dudes changed as soon as they got the pussy. They do what it takes to get it, but not what they need to do keep it. That's how I knew I had a good man on my team. They don't make 'em like him anymore.

When the massage ended I was handed a La Perla bag and instructed to put on the contents in it. As I sat on the massage table with my legs dangling off the side like a little kid. I dug inside the bag and came out with a cute little black nighty with crotch-less panties with the rhinestones to match.

I did a little tease while I put it on. Everything fit perfectly and he kept saying how good I looked in it. I made my way over to the chair and sat down. He started to feed me the chocolate covered strawberries and the rest of the fruit. As I ate them he put them on other parts of my body.

He left a chocolate trail right down to the best piece of chocolate. Me. He caressed me. Teased me. Touched me. Kissed me. Licked me. Bit me. He had me so aroused I was ready to take the dick from him. *Damn, this nigga got me going.* He had this fur looking throw on the floor next to the chair.

I missed it before because of everything else. He moved the massage table out of the way, turned the fireplace on. Next he gently laid me down on top of the blanket and boy did it feel good against my half naked body.

He continued his field day with my body with every touch being oh so passionate. He was rough yet smooth at the same time. His hands explored every inch of me. I took it all in and enjoyed every minute of it.

He grabbed my hips and pulled me toward him. I was on my hands and knees at that point with my back arched just right. He began to enter me from behind. He took his time and was very gentle. Slow and easy.

Just the penetration alone had me on the verge of an orgasm. He went in and out with long steady strokes. He was hitting it like a champ.

He put his hand in my hair, grabbed it and pulled my head back to his. He whispered, "Mi love yuh, Karter." Just those four little words made my ass melt on the inside.

I was about to cum and so was he. We came together and what we shared made me feel as if I was on a whole different planet. I squirted all over him. It felt as if the feeling would never end. I was on cloud nine. We just laid there in each other's arms until we fell asleep.

We woke up hours later. It was early evening at that point. While we got the house back in order he informed me that I needed to get ready for the next event. The highlight of the evening.

"Yuh need to go and prepare yuh self," Judah said.

"Prepare? where we going?" I asked.

"Calm yuh self and go prepare." He replied and kissed me on my forehead. "Do as mi sah."

"Thank you for everything Judah. I love you so much!" I told him.

"Mi love yuh too, gurl." He kissed me. "Yuh deserve it all," he told me. "Now, come on mon. Ya slow. No extra time. Come. Come now," He said sarcastically.

"Yeah, yeah, yeah. I ain't that damn slow and I went to shower. When I was done I dried off and walked into his room. I made my way to the bed and there were several wrapped boxes and cute bags. I felt like a little kid. I loved getting new stuff and opening gifts.

I dug into the first bag from Crushers, a little boutique that I loved and the shit there was not cheap. It was a bad ass dress. I looked at the tag, but of course the price part was gone. I wondered why people, women especially, wanted to know how much gifts cost? Why couldn't we just be glad for the gift and keep it moving?

The next thing I opened was a wrapped box. When I pulled out all the items in that bag there was a pair of these spectacular nude strappy heels with a clutch with clear stones on the top right corner to match. I didn't know where the fuck we were going, but wherever it was I would be the coldest bitch in that joint.

Last, but certainly not least, there was a bag. There was a box inside and I opened it. There was an iced out Cartier watch. It almost blinded me when I saw it. Just after I opened it and viewed it, I ran straight to Judah's office where he was in front of the computer on the phone. I had the watch in my hand. I wanted him to help me try it on.

I turned his chair toward me, crawled in his lap, and kissed him all over. "Thank you, baby," I said in his ear in a seductive voice. "I love everything. Let me show you just how much." He gave no verbal response, he just simply looked at me with a slight smirk on his face.

I kissed him from his ear down until I reached below his belly button. I figured I may as well break him off. I was feeling freaky, anyway. All of that fire attention I was getting turned me on I had to give some back. I made sure I wasn't too abrupt because he was still on the phone. I could tell it was business by the way he was talking. I didn't need him for what I was about to do, anyway.

He had on a black tank and grey jogging pants. I made my way down to the elastic of his jogging pants. I pulled his semi hard dick out and placed my tongue right in the tip and lick all on it. I slobbed him down, starting to take more into my mouth with every lick.

His dick was fully erect at that point. I went up and down with my mouth and round with my tongue. One of my hands played with his balls while the other was stroking the shaft of his dick as I took him in and out of my mouth.

He tried to continue with the phone call he was on, but once I let the tip of his dick hit the back of my throat with no gag reaction he ended the phone call fast. I continued my head job.

I kept on, up and down, with my hand around his balls. I didn't miss an inch of his male parts. He was loving it. I went so hard that every time I took him in, my throat made a clicking noise. One of his hands was all in my hair and the other was gripping the arm of the computer chair he was sitting in.

I took care of him quick and it was so fucking intense. Just the thought of me pleasuring him got me aroused. He busted right in my mouth. I swallowed it. Got up and went straight into the room to hop in the shower.

He was stuck. I made my shower quick. I got dried off and started on my make-up and hair. While I was doing that Judah had taken his shower and was dressed long before I was. I had finally perfected my face, and my hair was on point. I was ready to slip into my dress.

When I had it and my shoes on, I did a once over in the mirror. I was hot. Looking, feeling, smelling like a million mutha fuckin dollars. My dress was teal blue, long with the lowest cut ever. It was cut all the way down to the small of my back so panties were not an option.

It hugged my hip and ass just right. It was just the right length, so you could still see my shoes when I walked. My shoes were simple, but bad as hell. They showed my toes, and strapped around the ankle.

"Yuh ready?" Judah yelled.

"YES," I yelled.

"Come now," He said.

I knew he was tired of waiting on me so I didn't say anything back I just made my way up front. When I made it to the kitchen where he was he had shot glasses on the counter filled with good ole Don Julio. Clear. Chilled. That was my drink. He picked one up and handed it to me.

"Cheers ta dem bday!" he said as we made another toast. We stood in the kitchen and took about three shots. Straight to the face. I was a G at that shit. By the time we made it down to the car I felt my drink sneaking up on me that fast. It doesn't take too long for tequila.

We took my car, but he drove. I was glad because I wanted to roll in my new whip. I had a wonderful birthday. Judah always treated me special. Judah always took care of me. I kept asking him where we were going, he just told me I would soon find out. "Relax yuh self and jus ride yuh hear," he said. "We soon reach."

We made it to our destination, which was this little bar and sushi place not too far from his loft downtown. We had a few appetizers and sipped on some drink and jaw jacked for a minute, and then I asked him, "So, what's next?"

"Who said its a next ting?" he answered my question with a question. I hated that shit. He knew it too that's the reason he did it so often. I replied.

"I know you and I know for damn sure we didn't get this fly to come here." I said to him.

"Yuh don know whatcha chat bout!!!" he said with a laugh.

"I do." I told him. "You know you like showing me off. Now, gimme some." We leaned toward each other and kissed. We drank some more and with that, we bounced. The shots were starting to catch up with me. That was for sure.

I opened the ashtray as soon as I got back in the car and fired up the joint. I hit it a few times, passed it, and just sat back and rode.

We hit a few corners. We made a quick stop over one of his partner's house. I didn't ask why., I just assumed it was to kill time until it was time to go to the club.

I sat in the car, finished the joint, and turned up the music. I was feeling myself. When he got back in the car he handed me a blue scarf and told me to put around my eyes and don't peek. I didn't ask anymore question or anything. I did what I was instructed to do and enjoyed the smooth ride I was on. I was high and tipsy. I couldn't wait to get to the club I was gone dance my ass off.

After we rode for what seemed like a long as time. I asked, "What is taking so long to get there?" "Gurl ya need ta chill. We soon reach," he replied. Finally, the car stopped. He directed me to stay put and he would come and get me out. I still couldn't take the scarf off. The suspense was killing me. I liked surprises but shit, what was we about to do. *Damn I wanted to know.*

My door opened, he grabbed my hand, and led me up to the mystery spot. He put my hands on what felt like a door knob and told me to push it as soon as I did he took the scarf off of my eyes. As soon as I took one step: S-U-P-R-I-S-E!!!!

Chapter Eighteen

I didn't even have my eyes open good. I didn't know what the fuck was going. I jumped back a few inches but Judah was right there to catch me from going too far. I wasn't expecting that. That caught me completely off guard.

Everybody ran up to me with hugs, kisses, and warm embraces. All kinds of friends and loved ones were there, from the job, some classmates from the beauty college, Sis and Jay, some of Judah's friends and even some of my clients.

I was so surprised to see Sis and Jay. I was in tears. It felt good to have people around me that really fucked with me. It was good to see them. I hugged her for a long time. After all the shit we had all just been through I was glad to see her on good terms.

There was finger foods and fruit trays along with the normal eats you have at a party. Let's not forget the rotel and chicken wings. Judah knew that was my favorite.

It was streamer, banners, a gift table, and balloons. There was so much alcohol it was ridiculous and not to mention the cake. It was so damn big it had a table of its own. It read: CONGRATULATIONS AND HAPPY BIRTHDAY Karter !!!! There were balloons and shit everywhere too.

I thought to myself, *Congratulation on what?* I was still high so I was a little stuck. *And, what building is this we are at anyway?*

Then, the weird client from earlier today came up to me and took me away from that thought. Her hair was banging if I may have said so myself. I was good.

"Hey, Tianna!" I said to her. "I see your hair is holding up good."

"Yeah it is," she said.

"That's cool. Glad you could make it," I told her.

"So, how does it feel?" she asked me.

"You know what I really don't feel any different." I responded.

"Naw……ha! That's funny," she said with this evil little smirk.   "I want to know how it feels to be with my man?" she said.

"Excuse me?" I said to her. I was taken aback. "What did you just say? Your man? Bitch please."

Now I was switching from cool, high, chill bitch mode, to I'm about to whoop this hoe ass mode. This bitch had a lot of fucking guts.

I wondered like who was she? Really? Was she some bitch Judah been fuckin? Ah HELL NA!!! I done laid this bitch hair out, too! Somebody about to get they ass beat tonight.

"Yeah, you heard me. MY MAN. Oh, that's right you think my name is Tianna. Na, baby girl, I'm Estelle," she said. "And tonight Judah is leaving with me."

Okay, I thought. This is the crazy fucking ex-girlfriend. Was she the bitch that burnt my car up? Is she the bitch that Harasses me and my man, plays on the phone and shit?

"So, you the crazy deranged bitch Estelle huh?!"

"That's right," she said with the shift of her hip. This bitch was crazy to own up to that title but hey, at the same time why not own your shit.

"If you leave here tonight with my nigga y'all both gone be in body bags!" I said. By that time I had gotten inches closer to her face. I sobered up really quick.

I was about to beat the brakes off a her. Who the hell did she think she was coming to my fucking party with that bullshit. She had me and life fucked up.

At this point we had a small audience around us. You know Black people once they see a crowd they find out why there is a crowd.

So of course, Judah made his way to see what the hell went on. As soon as he seen her, he said, "Bombaclad yuh doin ere?" He instantly got pissed off and it was all in his face.

"What do you mean? I am here for you," she said. "And I am not leaving without you. You know you should be with me not her. Judah I am sorry for everything. PLEASE, come back to me," she pleaded with him.

What the fuck is wrong with her? He turned to me and said, "Mi got dis." Then, he turns back to her. "Estelle, yuh need ta leave dem now. Mi found somebody dat mi happy wit. Move on now. Mi don wann yuh."

"Yuh fucked up wit mi. No come back. Now jus a go for yuh cause a scene in da place dem." He said to her.

She was heated. She looked like she wanted to rip his eyes out!!! Even though, he had the situation under control I had to intervene. She was not about to get the ups on my man and I was right there.

I told her ass, "Bitch, bounce!" I knew she would try and jump, so I had already taken my shoes off while she was talking to Judah.

She reached back and had her fist balled up, but the next thing I knew her ass was flat on the floor. Sis came from nowhere and hit that bitch with a two piece. All I could do was think, *WOW! She didn't even know what hit her.* I guess there had to have been some type of drama to top off the evening.

The shit was hilarious. Sis was a damn nut. She handled that nice and quick. She always had my back. I did want to get at least one off on the bitch, though. It was funny because she thought she was about to clown me and take my man on my birthday.

I called the po po and had them take her right outta there. She had violated the restraining order that Judah had against her. I was damn sure pressing charges against her crazy ass. I was convinced she had set my car on fire, played on my phone, and all the other shit that couldn't be explained. She was a person I would say needs to be in the nut house.

For the most part the party was back cracking again. We were kicking it. The DJ was the shit. He played all the hip music and he kept them spinning. He whined it down a little with the ole school joint **Computer Love** and everybody got they two step on. When the song was over Judah grabbed the mic and called for everybody's attention.

All of the guest gathered around and he motioned for me to stand beside him. I complied with my drink in hand. As I stood next to my wonderful man I tried to figure out what this was all about. *He must gon' start the happy birthday song off.* I almost forgot about that part of the party.

He first made a toast to me. "Big up ta mi gurl dem, Karter. Duh prettiest gurl alive! Mi hope yuh like yuh new spot dem." With that we all toasted and they started singing happy birthday to me. I cut the cake and passed out pieces.

They hugged and congratulated me to death. Then, I realized what he said. My new spot. I was in shock. After the crowd cleared from the area Judah grabbed my hand and walked me into another room.

We stood there face to face, staring at each other not saying a word. I took his face into my hands, and asked, "Is this really mine? You did all this for me?"

"Ya mon. Dis ere all fa yu gurl. Mi job is ta make yuh happy. Mi wuld give yuh de world if mi culd," he responded.

That was the sweetest thing I had ever heard. I was in tears. I was so outdone. I had so many emotions running through me I didn't know what to say.

I managed to get out, "Thank you Judah." I kissed him softly on his lips. And again. And again. "Now can you take me on a tour of my new spot?" I asked as I laid one more on him.

We went on the tour of the building, he went on to explain to me that he bought it for me free and clear. He explained that I could do whatever I wanted with it because it was mine.

The place was humongous. It was perfect, just enough space for me to put everything I needed to make it a full service salon. It even had an upstairs. I was overly excited. I couldn't wait to start the makeover process.

By the time the DJ left so did the last guest. We walked through my salon one more time while still fucked up. I shared with him some of my ideas and explained how I wanted to change this and that, but half of that shit didn't come out right because I could barely walk straight.

As I was going down the steps and reached the last one, well I thought it was last one. I fell flat on my ass in my pretty ass dress. It was so fucking funny and we both fell out laughing uncontrollably! We were fucked up.

I got up and took my drunk as over to a chair. I sat down. Judah walked around to check the bathrooms and the back door. He came over and stood in front of me. He placed his hands on my face, but I pushed his hands away and grabbed at his pants. I looked up at him and we both smiled.

He knew what the deal was. He knew what I wanted because he wanted it, too. He took his gun out of the holster and put it on the table next to us as I unfastened his belt. I then unbutton his slacks, and then unzipped them. His pants fell to the floor. I started to massage his dick through his boxers. It started to harden with every touch.

I pulled his boxers down and let them hit the floor as well. I started kissing the head of his dick while I stroked his shaft. I let it fully enter my mouth. I went around on the head with my tongue.

My head went up and down on his dick. As I slobbed him down all I could hear was the noise my lips made against his dick, him moaning and clicking noise my throat made every time he hit the back of it.

I played with his balls and kept sucking. I was feeling freaky as hell. I didn't know if it was all the attention I had gotten all day, the fact that he got this building for me, or the fact that I just like to give him head because I loved the shit outta him.

As I continued to perform my fire head job my pussy was wet and throbbing at that point. I wanted the dick. Bad. I started to really get into it. I continued to put his dick as far back in my throat as it would go. My gag reflexes were very well controlled. The moans got louder as he grabbed a fist full of my hair.

I could tell he was about to come, but I didn't want him to, not just yet. I stopped, but I wasn't done. I had to get mine's off, too! I got up and sat him down in the chair. His dick was so hard it could cut a diamond. Right at that moment, I needed it to stay that way.

Just as he finished putting on the condom, I lifted my dress and straddled him. My panties were already off and he slid his nice hard long dick right in my wet warm oozing pussy. Damn this nigga felt good! He went right to work. Judah got busy and the shit was the best.

The sex was already fire, but when you added to it the fact that we were both tow the fuck up and feeling freaky as hell, there was no comparison. We fucked in the middle of my new salon on my birthday! We went at.

We changed positions, broke a sweat, busted a condom and all. We fucked like that until we both came, which we did it at the same time. That was the shit. I loved it when we did that. I loved our sex and I loved him.

Just as we started to let go of the embrace with one another, we heard this loud as BANG. It was almost like a gunshot or something big and hard had fallen to the ground.

Judah immediately jumped and went toward the table where his gun was; at the same time I dove to the floor from on top of him. I got out of the way from whatever the fuck that was and him getting to his heat.

Before I knew it I was being pulled to my feet by my hair while I had a glock 45 holding an extended clip and laser beam up under my chin by a masked man, telling me to shut the fuck up. I was trying to pull away from him and fight him off, but of course he was much stronger than me. On top of the fact it was a gun to my fucking chin.

It was three of them all together. At the same time a different nigga had a Mac 10 to Judah's head while the other nigga stood next to him, pointing a got damn AK-47 with a 100 round drum at him. Judah had his pants still around his ankles. I looked over at the table and his gun was still lying there. My heart dropped. Fuck!!! I said to myself. He wasn't able to get to it in time. The niggas came in too quick. They were in all black from head to toe. Only thing that could be seen was their eyes.

Who were these dudes, and what the fuck did they want with us? I didn't know what the fuck to do. I was so scared. I called out his name, "Judah!" The intruder that had me by the hair grabbed it tighter put the gun in my mouth, and said, "Bitch, I said shut the fuck up!" I didn't make another sound after that. I was sobered up. There I was in the most vulnerable state ever and so was my man. I couldn't take these dudes. I couldn't fight them off. *How in the hell was I about to get out of this one?* I asked myself.

The dude with the big gun stood there, looking at Judah. Mind you he still had his pants around his ankles. "Mi pull up mi pants mon." He said to the dude that stood directly next to him with the Mac 10. It also had an extended clip. He looked at the dude who had me for direction before he answered.

Whoever these niggas were they was not playing with us. *Who the fuck was these niggas?* I thought to myself. I knew they wanted us alive or we would have been dead already. At least that was what I tried to tell myself as a means of comfort. The dude that had me answered with a simple head nod.

"PULL 'EM UP NIGGA!!!! AND HURRY YO BITCH ASS UP!" said the guy with the Mac 10. Judah slowly pulled his pants up not to make any sudden moves. Just as he looked up at me, the one that was holding the gun on me grabbed me by the back of my neck and put the gun right to my temple.

He said to Judah, "If you even think about making a power ranger move I'm a blow her motha fuckin head smooth the fuck off, NIGGA! Get froggy if you want to, dis bitch gone be dead in here!" Judah looked at him with pure hate and disgust. Judah looked like he wanted to kill that nigga. Hell I'm sure he actually did. I had never seen him like that before though.

Judah was cool and calm. He hardly ever showed emotion. Especially temper. He didn't even argue with me. If I tried to pop off he would get real quiet and or walk the fuck away. He was not big at "war" as he called it with me. He said he did enough of that with how he made his living.

I tried to tell him with my eyes *baby just do what they say*, but I couldn't. I wanted him to know that no matter what happened I loved him. I wanted him to know that if I didn't make it, he made me one of the happiest women in the world.

I wanted him to know that I would love to spend the rest of my life with him. I wanted him to know all those things and a hell of a lot more. But, that wouldn't happen right then. It may have never been able to happen.

I screamed again. I couldn't help it. The dude that had me, slapped me across the face. It hurt like hell. It felt like a heater was just sat on the side of my face. It felt like it was bleeding, but I wasn't able to touch it to tell for sure.

I was still scared, but I was also mad as hell that this dude had just hit me across my face. This is some bullshit. I wanted to just bust this muthafucka dead in his mouth like he had just done me. As I was bent over I thought to myself, *okay Karter, get it together think girl think.*

As I tried to give myself a pep talk they had forced Judah to his knees by beating him for trying to get at the dude for slapping me. He was spitting blood at that point.

His shirt was still off. Sweat was all over his body. His eye was beginning to swell. His lip was busted. He was fucked up. All he had on were his pants that were now pulled up and his iced out chain with no emblem.

He kneeled there, looking at all of them. The look that I saw in his eyes was getting worse. It was like he was about to turn into the hulk or something. I could see his chest rise with every breath and he started to sweat even more. I knew he was contemplating his next move.

At that point big gun dude, who hadn't said a word the entire time, started talking to the nigga that was clearly in charge.

"A bro. Let's off they asses now," he said to him in this muffle voice.

"We gon' do this shit how I wanna do it and that's that. You do what the fuck I say," head nigga said.

Just as those last words came out of his mouth my heart dropped to my stomach and I got the nastiest taste in my mouth. That was that nigga Enoch. I thought to myself.

What the fuck?! That was some wild shit. My mind started racing. *How long had he been in Atlanta? How did he know I was there? Did he know he was positive? Did he really burn my fucking car up?*

Either was he had found me. I knew it would be a matter of time. He fucking found me. I should have stuck to my plan. I was supposed to find him first and fucking knock his ass off. Instead this nigga had found me and my man.

An overwhelming feeling of guilt settled over me. I looked over at Judah and I realized I had put the most important person in my life in harms way. This shit was all my fucking fault. Some bullshit behind Enoch.

But was it really behind Enoch? No. That shit was behind my actions. I took Enoch's money and dope. I was strung out on dope and did anything to get more of it. Not Judah. I took shit that I wanted from people. Not Judah. Even though I thought of no one but myself when I took that shit from Enoch, it sure has seemed to affect everybody around me.

Judah didn't deserve this shit. He didn't deserve any of it. On top of it all he didn't know why Enoch was so adamant about getting at me in this way.

He probably just thought Enoch was crazy like Estelle and wanted me back. I knew one day I would have to explain it all to him. I hoped so bad I would get the chance. I didn't care the outcome as long as I could see him alive again.

I started to contemplate how I was going to get us away from these niggas. Better yet, how we were going to kill them. I knew the only way this would end would be by death. Them or us. Hell with Enoch, it was every man for himself. He sure was out for him. Period. He would stop at nothing but he had to be stopped.

Enoch and the big gun dude started going back and forth. They went at it about what the next move should be and how the shit wasn't a part of the plan.

Judah looked for his opportunity, but the dude with the big gun never moved from his position. I got bold, though. I was even more pissed. This nigga done found and kidnapped, me and my dude.

"Enoch!?," I said with a you got me fucked up kinda tone. I don't know why shit with people surprised me, especially when it came to him. I turned my head toward him when I said it.

He had me so close to him I could smell his breath. All conversation stopped. The room fell quiet. The tension even thicker. The suspense and fear grew even more.

Chapter Nineteen

He pulled his mask off, and started screaming at me, "Yeah, BITCH! It's ME! SEE! SEE!" He was all in my face. He got even closer in that instant. He was so close I could feel his spit and warmth of his breath. Judah tried to get on his feet and the yes nigga kicked him in the back of his legs and started beating him again with the gun. I yelled, "STOP! STOP! LEAVE HIM ALONE!"

I turned to Enoch and asked him why he was doing that? I asked him what he wanted with us? "I want all yo niggas money and after I get it, I'm a make his bitch ass watch me torture you! Then, maybe kill y'all both for the shit you gave me! Bitch!" he said with this ugly ass mug on his face.

He pulled something small out of his pocket, turned it over, and emptied a white powdery substance on the back of his hand and sniffed it off.

He looked at me the entire time as if he was daring me to move. *This nigga was still a fucking stoner,* I said to myself. I wasn't surprised because at this point not too much of what Enoch did or had done shocked me anymore.

I tried to process the fact that he said he wanted to kill me and my nigga. It also dawned on me at that time that this nigga said "the shit I gave him". *What the fuck?!* I thought the nigga was pissed and out to get us because of the shit I took from Bunny's house.

He had to be high out of his fucking marbles. He was delusional. All this was because he convinced himself that I had given him the package. Hell naw! I thought. He was the undercover brotha. He was the one out here screwing this dude and that girl. Not me!! He had me and life all fucked. I was NOT positive.

But fuck was I? I did have to continue to be tested. I knew that. And another thing I would have to explain to Judah. How would I explain that to him along with everything else? I didn't have a choice though. That was for sure.

I knew Enoch was still pissed about me taking his shit. *Fuck him, though!!! I was the one that got the shit, anyway!!!* Then, I started to wonder if he was upset about the fact that I caught his ass in the act of fucking another man. As all this was going on they had gagged and tied Judah up.

Then, he ordered the big gun, nigga to gag and tie me up as well. At the end, he said, "I'm tired of hearing the stupid bitch talk." But, don't think I didn't put up a struggle.

Don't think I was just about to be a yes bitch and LET him do shit to me. I started hitting and kicking. Scratching and grabbing, but to no avail. I was like fuck it. They gone kill me, kill me but FUCK ENOCH and his crew!

I was then forced to sit in a chair to which my feet were tied to. My hands were tied behind my back. It wasn't regular rope they used. It was a zip tie type. Hard to penetrate and hard to wiggle out of. Judah and I both had that around our hands and feet.

As I sat in the chair with a damn scarf tied around my mouth, I looked at Judah and he looked back at me. I almost started crying, but I knew I couldn't let Enoch see a tear fall from my eyes. I knew I had to show no weakness at all in that situation. I held that shit in.

Enoch came up behind me and bent over, so that his lips were right by my ear. He reached something out of his hoodie pocket in the front. He never put his mask back on. He didn't give a fuck at that point who saw or recognized him. The cat was out of the bag when I caught his voice and called his bitch ass out.

He pulled out a needle. My heart started to race more. I started to sweat. I didn't know what was in the needle, but I knew it was some type of narcotic. The shit I had been so desperately addicted to.

The shit that he controlled me with for so long. The shit that I had finally overcome needing in my life. And then there I was watching Enoch holding a fucking needle full of it waiting to take me right back to that place again. He used the drugs to control me when he had me strung the fuck out. And he was going to do the same thing now.

He started to speak to me. "I got some dope for you. I know you want it. You been around this nigga like you a good clean girl. You is a fuckin dope head, BITCH!" He laughed. "You is a feign!!" He keeps badgering me. "You been trying to put on a front like you don't use drugs." "Ha!!! Yeah, okay."

He kept talking. "The word on the street is you been off the dope since you been here. When I heard that shit I said that weak bitch can't kick no dope habit!" All three of them laughed.

"It don't matter now, though 'cause I got some shit that gone have you right back feigning!!!" He had been holding the needle the whole time. Next thing I knew he pulled my hair, making my head lean all the way to the side.

He said, "I'm a put this shit right in your veins." I tried to move and avoid it, but no way to. He had ahold of my hair with so much force I couldn't move it. My head all the was leaned back so my face was looking toward the ceiling. I closed my eyes as if that would block what I knew was coming. I felt his fingers touch my skin. I began to must have found a vein and he began to administer the drug.

Next thing I felt after the sharp poke with something cool going through me. Before I knew it I was high as fuck and could barely control my body. I wasn't able to move anyway after being gagged and bound. But, it just felt like I was super heavy and had so much weight on me that I wasn't able to do anything.

They faced me toward Judah. I couldn't read his expression anymore. He had a flat effect on it. He was showing no emotion whatsoever.

It didn't help that I was getting higher and higher by the second it felt. I didn't know if I was still seeing things. I didn't know if my senses were still working properly.

I wondered what was going through Juda's head. I was sure he was processing everything like I was. And I was sure he was confused about all the shit Enoch was talking. I hoped liked hell that my past hadn't fucked up the potential future I had with him.

I was pissed, but I couldn't do anything about it. I had been clean all this time and this mutha fucka came along over some bullshit and pumps me full of some fucking dope. I had been getting my shit in order and living legit. I had finally found a decent man. But Enoch just wouldn't let me be.

That nigga was on nothing, but straight bullshit. It was like he had to control me and my life somehow. He didn't care about the fact I struggled with the cravings from my addiction every day. He didn't care about the fact I had been clean for a while. He wanted to control me and have me strung out just like he was.

Everything was so heavy and hard to process. It was like my mind was working extra hard, but still I could barely think. All I wanted to do was close my eyes. They were heavy as hell too. Whatever he had given me, had me gone.

I was so helpless in my own body and thoughts I started to get frustrated, and then angry. Finally, I could no longer overcome the drug and I began to give in unwillingly to it. As I sat there time seemed to move extremely slow. I tried my best to stay awake, but I felt myself dozing off no matter how hard, I tried I couldn't fight it.

I nodded off and my head fell and I yanked my neck back up. I opened my eyes and things were blurry. I somehow managed to focus and when I did I seen Enoch beating the shit out of Judah. I was gagged and tied up so my yells sound like muffle grunts. They were low and rather soft because I was so fucking weak.

I began to cry and next thing I knew I was out again. *What the hell is going to happen to him? Are they going to beat him to death?* I felt a sharp pain in my head. One of the intruders had yanked my head back up by pulling my hair. He told me I needed to stay my bitch ass awake so that I could watch them beat the shit out of my man.

I kept my eyes closed. I didn't want to see that shit. I didn't wanna see my man get beat half to death. The thing was I knew. I knew Judah well and telling them where and how they could get money was not going to happen.

I don't know what the fuck they thought, but he was a solid nigga. He would rather die than give in. He knew that when that type of shit happened, they were gone kill you rather you told or not. He was not going to fold.

Just as I felt the grip of my hair let go and my head fell forward again, I heard gunshots. I didn't even open my eyes I just sat there with my head bowed. I didn't wanna see them shooting Judah.

I didn't wanna see the love of my life dead. I could not bare the sight of him that way. But then, it was much more commotion than I heard throughout this whole ordeal. I forced my head up and my eyes open.

I saw Enoch and one of his boys taking cover and shooting toward the door. I seen Judah laying on the ground beaten badly, but still breathing. I also see one of Enoch's boys, lying face down in a puddle of blood. I had no idea who they shot. And I didn't know who had laid that nigga out like that either.

I wasn't in the position to see the direction they were shooting in. It seemed I was in the crossfire, though. I knew I needed to get out the way. I was still really heavy and sluggish. I wanted to move, but I couldn't. I heard nothing, but gunshots. The man that laid dead in his pool of blood was the intruder that carried the gun with the 100 round drum.

I couldn't see at all who was shooting at Enoch. I seen one of the other intruders shooting over my left shoulder. I didn't wanna get hit in the crossfire but I couldn't move. Judah was still out but I didn't want him to get hit either. I started to think again but it was still cloudy and fuzzy but I knew I needed to get out of the way and get low.

I took some deep breaths and thought hard. I took all of my energy and body weight to tip over the chair. I leaned to the right and with much force I could muster up.

The chair finally tipped and I landed on my right shoulder. I thought I would hit the ground hard, but I hardly felt it. Probably the drugs.

I opened my eyes once I hit the ground. Enoch ran toward me. He was still shooting. When he reached me he got down and grabbed me by my arm. I still heard gunshots even though he wasn't shooting any longer.

I still had no idea who they were coming from. He couldn't get me undone from the chair without getting shot, so he dragged me in the chair across the room toward the back.

He just used me as a human shield. He wanted to ensure he didn't get shot. He only cared about him. But that was obvious or else he wouldn't have even been there, at that time, doing that shit.

He had put my chair back on all fours and was sliding the chair across the floor as he was shooting over my shoulder. I got turned around and was now facing toward the gunfire.

The gun fire was coming from the front entrance area and it was Judah friend RG! *What the fuck was he doing here and why did he stop shooting?* It was like since he saw it was me he didn't take another shot. They started to yell back and forth.

Enoch screams to him, "Keep shooting, pussy. I don't give a fuck if you hit her or not." He looked at me with this look of confusion. He had a clear view of the entire set up and situation.

The salon building was in a row of other building/businesses. There was no side door because there were business on both sides of the salon. Enoch and his partner continued to shoot at RG.

He took cover behind the front desk reception area. That was one of the few things that were in the place. I think it used to be a daycare or massage parlor because it was so many rooms. But, where the party was and where we then stood, was the main area of the spot.

Enoch eased his way backward with the friend on some type of communication devices stating "It's that time." I had no clue what that meant and no idea what type of device he was on. I still could hardly process my thoughts and I was still a little heavy. But, I was starting to be less groggy.

The friend let off a few shots but they all should have been out of ammunition at that point. I opened my eyes as I was being dragged in the chair to the back door and I saw Juda in a pool of blood just like Enoch's friend. I didn't see any movement, his chest rising nothing.

My heart sank and I felt sick to my stomach. I was devastated and I could clearly see he was dead. That was some bullshit. They killed my nigga. They had taken my future. They had taken the one person who meant the world to me. I sort of just gave up then. My heart was gone.

We reached the backdoor and Enoch picked me up in the chair. We exited and a black Benz minivan pulled up with the passenger side, facing us and the sliding door opened. I saw RG running toward us, shooting, and then he just stopped. He must have run out of ammo because he still had his gun pointed toward the van.

They didn't even try and shoot back. I was literally thrown in the side door and the other guy hopped in the front. He never took his mask off. I heard the doors shut as the van sped off.

I was still in shock behind my nigga. I couldn't wrap my mind around any of what happened. I was kidnapped and drugged by my crazy ass ex-boyfriend and I had no idea where they were taking me and what they were going to do to me.

To be continued................

Thank you for reading! We hope you enjoyed it. Please be sure you leave a review on our website: Eclecticpublishingllc.com and Amazon.

Also be on the lookout for the next volume of Hustle Made series. Coming Soon!!!!!!!!